A FREE gift
from Author STEVE WINDSOR

What do you give away for FREE inside the book that you are giving away for FREE?

I had a major dilemma figuring this one out. But I bartered a couple of favors and twisted my author friend, Lise Cartwright's, arm until she agreed to record the audio version of STEG for your listening pleasure.

To download the audiobook version of STEG go to

http://vixenink.com/steg-audiobook/

Thank You.

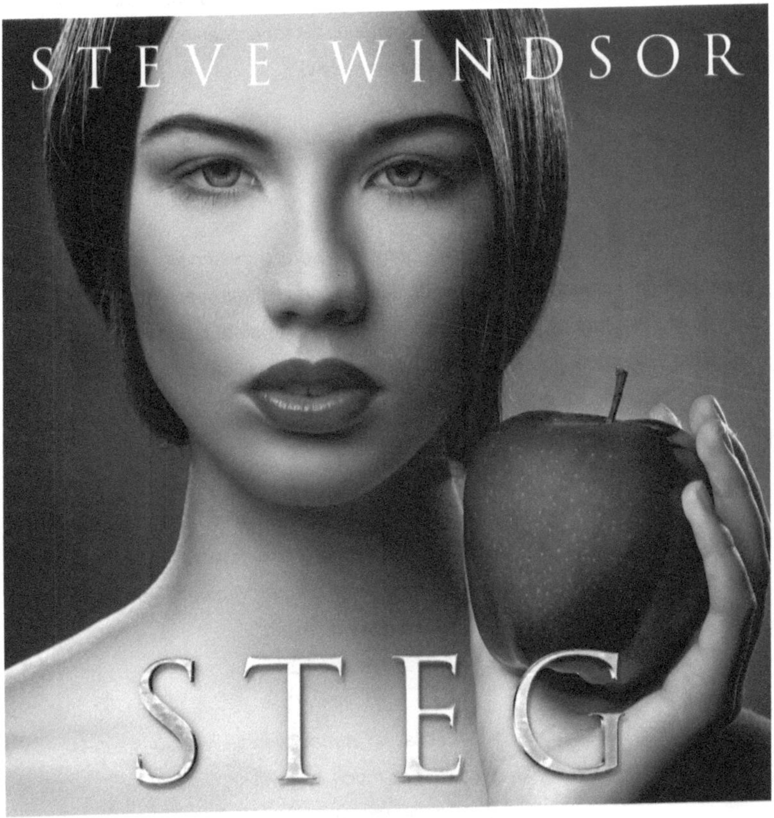

Praise for the novels of
Amazon Bestselling Author Steve Windsor

STEG

(PROLOGUE)

STEVE WINDSOR

VIXEN INK

This is a work of fiction. Names, characters, places, and incidents either are the product of the author's imagination or are used fictitiously, and any resemblance to actual persons, living or dead, business establishments, events, or locales is entirely coincidental. The publisher does not have any control over and does not assume any responsibility for author or third-party websites or their content.

STEG

A VIXEN ink book/Published by arrangement with the author

Copyright © 2015 by STEVE WINDSOR

Cover design by:

Steve Windsor - stevewindsor.com

ISBN-13: 978-0692392669
ISBN-10: 0692392661

To new beginnings

STEG

(PROLOGUE)

LIFE

MIDWAY INTO THE rain of rocks, I fell to my knees and couldn't rage my way back standing. I felt a huge crack as a rock blasted the base of my back and ruptured the lowest disk in my spine. Then everything below my waist went limp. I slumped to the side, done . . . but far from dead.

Ravens in the grandstands raged and rocks flew and some of them hit me, but many of them didn't. I slumped on my side, watching the ones that missed, thinking, *You've missed me, you miserable moronic flying monkeys.*

I coughed out a laugh and spit blood, and it covered a rock that *hadn't* missed its mark. The rock lie beneath my rage-red blood, truth spat and spilled over it.

After a time that seemed longer than my life in Eden's Great Garden, I grew numb and could no longer hear word nor whacking rock. The sound of rain droplets of rock was to be the last thing I would ever hear . . . and then one final star exploded into my face and my short time in that world . . . faded me back to the black.

My last thought—it was and still is the only logical question—drifted through my mind as the darkness surrounded me, *Why?*

Five eternities ago—ten thousand years if you mark the minutes as a Man-monkey does—there were two celestial sisters. They were ancient beings, the Lords Almighty of Creation. Born out of the blackness of the eternities, forged from the fire of the sun and grown from the firmament of the great Gardens of the galaxies. Shaped like clay and burned and baked in the great kiln of the cosmos, they were thrust into being by powers beyond even their comprehension.

Life, the youngest of the two, was imbued with the power of ten billion lightning bolts to spark life from the nothingness and bring starlight to the eternities. She was a whispering white soul, so bright an angelic being as to outshine all the stars.

As a god of the sky, the first God of what would become the heavens, Life was imbued with near-transparent wings and feathers, and she wailed the voice of wisdom itself. She viewed the nothingness through beautiful black orbs of benevolence—the eyes required for a god to see through the black. Life was eternal.

The nothingness—the black—was all there was then. It had always been and always would be. A dark place that all angels and gods escaped to in times of tumultuous trouble. Back to their beginning they would hide and be reminded of Life's might.

Life's first entrusted task, with all that might at her disposal, was to split the nothingness in two. She would create the eternal light of the sun to separate the unknown—the warm blanket of the darkness— from the white hot truth of the day. Without Life there would be only black.

With her wings intertwined tightly behind her, Life's mark was that of the bright orange light of the sun she would create. It would become the warmark of her followers in a Heaven yet to be.

Eden was the eldest of the two siblings, though time and its passing don't occur as you may believe. For everything that has happened will happen, and every tomorrow was born in a yesterday you have already lived. This was the Word that I knew. And it was also the Word of the great God, Eden—the Protector of the very first eternity.

Eden was born of the firmament. A bright green god, grown from the Garden of the galaxy to nurture and rear nature itself. As the mother of all natural things, hers was the task and responsibility to seed the soil, and then give that seed the water and warmth it needed to birth and raise life.

Eden was to be the queen of the woodcut line of archangel fairies, beings whose sole purpose was warmth and wonder and growth and goodness. Most of the descendants of Eden were lushly-colored, emerald-winged waifs, more suited to watering than war. Yet they were not without talons and teeth.

Eden's wings, tucked tightly behind her jade-feathered back, spoke of her garden as yet unborn. And they whirred like a hummingbird's as she flitted about, smiling at the wonders of the eternities.

When she stopped hovering long enough to alight on a perch, her wings formed the four-leaf clover—deep shamrock hearts, tips all touching each other—the warmark of the followers of Eden. Though, as I remember it, Eden liked to refer to them as the marks of "love and luck, and life and living," her promise of a "world of wonder" mark.

As Eden was the eldest, the cosmos ordained that she would be the Protector of the first eternity—she would be God. It was to be the eternity of the great Eden, the beginning of new life in the gardens of the galaxies. The great Gardens of Eden would be breeding grounds for all the creatures and beings that she would birth from the firmament of all the earths in the galaxies of time.

It was Life's duty to shine down upon those seeds with her godly bright light. Together, she and Eden would bring existence into being.

Since the dawn of this first eternity, and in every eternity since, sisters . . . disagreed. Life and Eden were no exception. Their very first dispute would set the heavens on a trajectory of oppression and misery that neither of them could have predicted, and only one of them was remotely equipped to survive.

As Protector of the first eternity, Eden decreed that she would populate her very first garden with beings in her and her sister, Life's, own images. She would pluck a single citron strand of her hair and create the mother of all men, Woman. Life would send a great Day Star serpent, a wise and knowing sage, cut and created from the beautiful, twisting white twine of Life's own locks.

And thus, Eden's very first daughter was "born"—her sole child—Lilith. And with the knowledge of the light of her Day Star to guide her, Lilith was stripped of her angelic wings and cast down into the Garden of Eden . . . to begin creation.

Woman and wisdom would guide the Garden through its first eternity. Or so it was thought. . .

Since Eden needed a way for Woman to fertilize her seed—be fruitful and multiply—she decreed that when Lilith arrived in the Garden, she would carve out a slice of herself—a being born of her own flesh, blood and name—to be created as "Man" to stand and tend the garden by her side, making sure no harm came to Woman and her omniscient snake.

Me? . . . How does all this intertwine with my own story of being cast into the pit of darkness and damnation? *I* . . . was my god's all-knowing snake—a being of perfect beauty—an expression of my God's own glory, knowledge and power. And I was sent to Eden's Garden to advise, assess, and "address any issues that might arise," if I remember it correctly. As I vowed to tell you the truth, in point of fact . . . I was Life's garden snake—a godly spy.

None of this information was my ally at the time, as I was yet to be created. A fact that would soon change.

In the Bible, the wages of sin are death. Throughout his eternity, Man has suffered the consequences of this part of the Word. It is what separates him from gods . . . from *the* God—the Protector of the current eternity. Though you've misinterpreted so much, I feel I must tell you that there are many gods, I being one of them.

Some people call us angels, but if a god is an all-powerful, vengeful and unforgiving creature, to those who purport to understand and bastardize the Word, we angels are gods by any other name.

And one thing you may be aware of, is that gods don't suffer consequences. They—we make rules—our covenants—for those whom we preside over and protect. It is an ironclad pact of protection, penance and punishment if need be. A parasitic relationship that serves primarily to place the powerful above their people. However, let me assure you—Heaven, Hell, or Eden creating her great Garden—sooner or later, sin touches every god. I was no different.

You know me by a hundred names—Day Star, Dal—the Dark

Angel of Light, the devil Lived, Lucifer, Lion, and even Liar. But before all of those, before I was cast from the Garden and flown into the pit, my Lord named me Steg. And I was an angel . . . as magnificent as any god.

As the highest covering archangel in Heaven, it was my task to guard the covenants of my Protector—my true God. To accomplish that task, I had to speak truth to power. And though this is not my testament—the statement of repentance of the great liar, Lucifer—this is the story of how mortal sin touched me . . . and the eternal consequences I am condemned to for it. This is the truth of my fall from my God's grace. And this is the truth you don't know about the sin and treachery in Eden's precious Garden. May Life nail me to a cross and *burn* me if I lie as I tell it.

LUST

— I —

I AWOKE SURROUNDED by darkness but bathed in the light of a. . . I had but one thought: *Who is this beautiful creature before me?*

The angel—I felt that was her kind—hovered above me. Her wings were barely noticeable as they buzzed to a transparent white blur. And she gazed at me through beautiful onyx eyes, as dark as the black nothing that was my memory of anything before that day.

I stared into her eyes. "Lovely," I said softly.

She smiled back. "As angel's own blue eyes are as beautiful and as close to ice as I dared make them. Any brighter and they would have approached a white, rivaling my own feathers. Yet I am eternally grateful for the compliment." Her voice felt wonderful to me and I drank it into my ears as my eyes drank in her beauty.

I raised up an arm to cover my face from her growing brightness. Then I lifted my legs individually, feeling into my new understanding of . . . *life?* That thought was deep in my mind. Somehow, I knew she had put it there.

She held up her hands in front of her and smiled. "Life!" she shouted. "Are we not wondrous?"

My body was bare and a slightly reddish shade of . . . I wanted to say "sun" for some reason. "What am I?" It was the very first question I had.

"Mmmm," the white angel spoke, but I had no understanding of it. For as she spoke, she glowed and shined so brightly that I covered my eyes and looked away. Then she laughed and her voice was more beautiful than she looked. She sang in a long comforting moan that worked its way into my ears, soothing and caressing my mind. "You are simply perfection," she spoke more clearly this time. "For I, the great God, Life, have created you. And you will be the sun of the morning that I shall create after that."

I smiled. "Shall I please you?" I asked. I could not explain it, but that is what I wanted most desperately.

Her wings slowed to a flutter. "Ah, my beautiful Day Star," she said, "you are the most pleasing piece of this prophetic day. And you will most certainly please me"—she lowered her hands and clasped them in front of her—"until the day that you die. May we pray that that day never comes."

I had no idea at the time what dying was, or why the day of my birth could be associated with a feeling that the word *prophetic* invoked within my . . . soul. I felt that wasn't quite the correct word. But it touched as deeply into me as the one she had put in my mind before it.

Before I could think further about it, a voice spoke from behind me, "Your serpent is beautiful." It was as glorious a sound as my white angel's moaning had been, more so I only dare say now. "I am so very proud of you, sister. No finer a feathered friend to guide Lilith, could I have imagined nor set eyes upon."

I turned toward the voice and nearly fell to my knees. Something attached to the back of my waist flipped and whipped wildly, and then my skin prickled and hardened to steel scales, and then long spikes jutted from my fingers and toes. "What?" I shouted, spinning around to try and face the lashing assailant. But it was no use and try as I did, I could not control it. "Who attacks me on the day of my own birth?" I shouted. "Who could I have offended in such a small turn of time as this?"

My own grandness spread wide and strong to my sides. The limbs were huge and covered in red steel, and each glowed bright crimson as I stretched them to their full width. "What are"—I grabbed at the whip behind me—"what is it?"

My fluttering white angel laughed a little. She pointed at the tip, whipping wildly behind me. "That is angel's own tail"—she motioned her arms toward my sides—"and *they* are your glorious wings. With them you shall dwell eternally in the throne room of my Heaven, in the very presence of your God. And you shall not know an enemy in any of the heavens that would dare attack you . . . lest they perish at the lightning from mine own hand!" She glanced behind me with an indignant look on her face. I would come to recognize the expression well, but had no notion of at the time.

Looking back, I know the gaze was meant for Eden, but at the time I didn't care. My Lord knows . . . I should have.

She returned her black-eyed stare to me. "As I've brought you forth from the nothingness, out of the bondage of the black, I shall be your Lord . . . your God. And you shall have no others before me."

A chill went through me and my wings shook and shuddered. I looked at them. *Wings*, I thought. And I smiled back at her.

She was so sure of my place beside her. Her words should have struck fear in me as remembering them does now, but they . . . comforted me. Though I remained bewildered as to the very nature and purpose of my existence, I was, for the moment, happy.

My wings softened and my—I had heavy armored red feathers over the entirety of my skin, save my face! I watched as they retracted and turned my body back to bare. The great spikes on my fingers disappeared as well. Then I felt the gaze of my own mother's beautiful black eyes and it warmed into. . . I touched my chest. *Hearts?* I thought.

My chest seemed to be where the feeling was centered. "What animal rages inside my chest?" I asked, having completely forgotten the other voice behind me.

"Thine own beating hearts," that forgotten voice said softly. "Two balanced beasts beneath angel's own breast."

Angel? I thought. *I am an. . .?* Though they had a design and mind of their own desires, I somehow managed to retract my wings behind my back. Then I turned, more carefully this time, to face the voice behind me.

Of the two of them, though I would have never thought possible. . . The greenish gaze of nature's own eyes stared at me, and the warmth and love that I felt in that moment simply cannot be described. For I had barely recovered from the wonder of meeting my Great Mother—my creator—when my eyes gazed upon nothing less than pure love.

The green glowing angel—I assumed she was another—reached out and touched my left breast and I relaxed at the warm feeling that penetrated my skin. "This one, beautiful Day Star, I've given to you. It shall guide you through darkness," the jade angel said. Then she turned to my Great Mother, now shining brighter than before. "And sister?" she said to her.

My Great Mother hesitated for an instant, before raising up her hand. And a long black spike slipped out from the tip of her first finger. She stabbed it into my chest as she spoke, "And this one shall be," her voice was louder.

Angrier, I thought even as the pain spiked into my chest. I winced and grabbed at the searing fire in my heart.

She continued, ". . .to bathe you in the white hot fire of the light!"

I heard a loud *CRACK!* Then everything around me—all I could see and feel—burst to brightness like ten billion stars exploding into existence. I was blinded and I fell to the ground.

The blackness split into two halves, and the bright half shined orange and white fire and blasted a heat I could barely withstand. So hot was my Great Mother's light that I curled into a ball on the ground and screeched and moaned at the pain the burning caused.

I felt the heat and fire sear into my feathers and my wings caught fire and smoked. Yet I could still hear both of them speaking as plainly as I recount it now. It would have been difficult not to, their voices reverberated and boomed so loudly, my ears rang inside my head.

"My Day Star shall be light!" my Great Mother's voice thundered.

I cringed at the pain her words brought and I continued to cower as I burned on the ground.

Then the lovely green god from yelled behind me, "And daughter Lilith shall be night!"

CRACK! Then the loudest, most thunderous sound of any I've heard since, split open my skull and exploded my body into ten billion streaking shards of bright light. And everything went back to the black before my birth.

— II —

THE LAST THING I remembered was waking up confused, meeting two beautiful angels, and then being blown apart into ten billion bursting white stars. I sat up and shook my head. The pain was simply. . . I looked at my appendages, certain they were nothing but seared flesh and singed feathers. I was more than shocked at what I saw.

I was no longer an angel, but . . . something else. Something I didn't recognize.

A voice—neither of my two angels—interrupted my confusion and the pain in my head. "You don't look all that knowledgeable and worldly to me, serpent," the voice said. "Yet my Great Mother informs me that you are to be my sage, so . . . pluck yourself from your bewilderment, snake, and let mine eyes drink in your wisdom."

My hearts pounded in my chest. My wings were missing and my skin was no longer red, replaced by a pale pinkish hue a mere few shades darker than my Great Mother's. I knew that was who she had been, and I also knew that she had sent me to that place to keep a watchful eye on this creature. "What . . . *are* you?" I asked. I knew many things and I understood that it was my own Great Mother who had taught them to me . . . somehow. Yet there were so many strange things—feelings I had no knowledge of.

The waif placed her hands on her hips. She was no angel. I cannot describe her to you and do justice to her form, though bare and breasted would be the efficient way to relate it. My eyes drank in her beauty as they had my Great Mother's.

She resembled my Great Mother and the beautiful sister who was with her, but she was somehow less . . . angelic. "Where are your wings?" I spoke without thinking. Though there was no shame, no guilt, no embarrassment at my appearance, nothing of the sins I would come to understand. "Have you lost them"—I reached back to make certain—"as I seem to have lost mine?"

"All-knowing," she scoffed, eyeing me up and down. "Your *wings*"—she cocked her head to the side as she spoke—"have been cropped, as has angel's own tail. Though that isn't what you are any longer. For we are not tasked with an angel's work. Ours is more humane labor than this."

Somehow, I knew my Great Mother had given me the understanding that this creature was speaking the truth. Yet, barely an infant in my knowledge of anything, I craved more. "Then what is my purpose here if not angel?" That I didn't understand.

She reached a hand down and helped me to my feet. Touching her hand was wonderful, though I believed I needed to guard those thoughts. *That* knowledge, my Great Mother had put into my mind unmistakably. "Certainly not the task of *Man*," she said. "For were I to create Man in *thy* image"—she looked away and the slightest laugh escaped her lips—"I should have nothing more beautiful to tend in my Mother's Garden. And of this, Eden would not be pleased. That is to say nothing of what her sister—" She turned back toward me, surprise barely concealed on her face, eyes bigger than what seemed natural to me.

I crossed my arms and simply looked at her.

Her eyebrows lifted slightly. "How rude of me," she said, shaking her head. "I am. . ." Then she hung her head and closed her eyes before opening them back up. The blue in them shined nothing but happiness into my hearts. "Forgive me. Your god's serpents are not the task of Eden's daughter." She seemed to be as well informed as I was. And yet. . . *Serpents?* I thought.

Despite my confusion, I smiled at her. For I knew ours would be a wonderful "working" relationship. I pointed around us at the lush greenery, slowly darkening as my Great Mother, Life, caused the sun to set. And Eden's Garden grew dim.

I understood the Garden, my Mother made certain of that. I also knew that this beautiful creature's name didn't matter. I was free, I was in the Garden and there was my God's work to be done. However, maybe out of politeness, or maybe curiosity at the details of my newest new world. . . Though that is a lie, because this creature's name was as important to me as the air I was breathing. "And does Eden's daughter wear name in nature?" I asked. Then I looked up at the darkening sky. "Let not my Mother's light darken before it falls from heaven-sent daughter's lips."

We stood in our bareness, neither aware of the other's. . . We had no word to describe our exposed skin. For certain, I didn't. We were beings sent and set to the purposes of our gods, never considering the consequences of what either of us was about to do.

She smiled. "I like you, serpent," she said. "Were this another eternity, I should think your task equal to my own. Yet, as this is Eden's eternity"—she touched her hands to her shoulder so gently that I shivered watching it—"and daughter *Lilith* shall birth her Garden's masters, I am set to task of purpose—the dawn of the people of

Woman."

"Lilith. . ." I let the breath from the word caress its way up from my chest and slip out of my mouth. Then I smiled at her, nodding my head as I did. "It's a fine name for a daughter of Eden," I said. Then I looked up at the darkening sky. "As fine as my Great Mother's sun on this eve."

Lilith looked up with me. "And yet my own Mother's half of the day hastens its arrival to save us from this scorching light. Only stars left to shine a hint that your Mother's bright was ever here." And with that, the Woman of Eden's Garden walked away. She brushed her hands across leaves and flowers as she sifted her loveliness into the depths of the greenery.

I followed as a pup would its mother. "And what of the dawn?" I called after her.

"On my second day in the Garden," she shouted back, "I shall create Man . . . and it shall be good."

I hastened my pace to catch up to her. Then I raised my voice, hoping she would slow and wait for me. "Then *I* shall bring the Son of the Morning to bear witness to it," I shouted after her.

Good? I thought. As I followed Lilith into the dark myrtle-covered undergrowth of Eden's glorious Garden, for some reason, good was not the storm my hearts felt brewing.

There were many magnificent things in the Garden. Some I understood implicitly and some that just were—neither needing me to nor caring whether I grasped their existence or not. Nature and her glory simply were . . . and some things were not.

The center of the Garden was as peaceful as the poppies that grew all around it, and I laid next to Lilith, lounging on my back underneath the sap trees. We listened to the cicadas *chirr-chirr-chirr* themselves into the dark of their "day." My God's stars winked at us as bright as they could. Ten billion pinpricks of twinkling truth shined down . . . just enough.

The two of us—the offspring of Eden and Life—were serenaded to sleep with our own private lullaby in our own personal Garden of Eden. Yet something inside me warned that by the very next day . . . that bliss would end.

Was I prepared for it? . . . That was my task.

That night, Lilith and I slept in warmth and comfort, caressed by the Garden's flora and fauna like a mother strokes her daughter's hair.

Not long after I fell asleep, my Great Mother, Life, visited me in my dreams. Though dream and reality intertwined, wrapping themselves around me like the slithering serpent my God created me to be.

Neither awake nor completely asleep when she appeared to me, Life shined so brightly that I feared she would wake Lilith from her own dreams, whatever they might be. Yet I knew not to protest, and for some reason I worried that the mere thought alone would be an unwelcome guest in my mind.

My Great Mother hovered over me—a knowing look on her face—and then she glanced at Lilith beside me. "I see you are . . . *embracing* your task"—she looked back at me and her black eyes shined—"rather well, young Steg."

I had never heard my own name from her lips, let alone felt it spoken in such a smooth and sensuous way. "And how long must I guard Garden's waif"—I motioned above us both to the sap trees, hovering overhead—"from ominous threat of dripping sweetness? For I wish only to return to my Mother's bosom for precious blessing, promised upon completion of my virgin task in her sister's glorious garden."

She smiled down at me—a downturned grin of goodness and godly approval. I grinned back, feeling her mind working its way into mine. Then we both looked at Lilith, slumbering peacefully not a stone's throw away.

Our eyes met even as my Great Mother's mind melted into mine. "I suppose I can ill-afford to leave my precious snake, filled with a virgin's vile venom, whilst slumbering next to my sister's precious prey," she said. "Of this, unavoidably, I've made you incapable of resisting. So . . . in order that you should honor your Great Mother and be relieved of such adulterous temptations, I come bearing gift of wifely wonder."

It was at that moment that something crept its way into my understanding, slithering its way inside my confidence and calm until I was suddenly aware of threats I had been ignorant of not moments before. I felt . . . guilt. Yet it was not for deeds done in deceit, but only the thought of them and the consequences for their . . . consummation. I glanced at Lilith, but turned my gaze back to Life as quickly as I realized what I was thinking.

She continued to smile down at me. Had she already read my thoughts? Clearly she had that power, but I hoped that my hesitation was misplaced. "Ahh," she said, "I see that I am correct in this assessment." Or possibly not, but were it not for her next action toward me, I might never have "known" my God as completely as would be required in order to survive her.

Life fluttered down on top of me and I felt a wondrous warmth beneath her shining light and wide-spread wings. It was not brightness so much as understanding and knowledge and truth, as I knew it at that time. And I must tell you that the sensations were exquisitely pleasurable and painful at the same time. In fact, distinguishing the difference was as difficult as it was to allow it to end.

When she was finished with me, I was as venomless a viper as any serpent—fangs faltering, still sunk deeply into freshly poisoned flesh —could be. "You are as delectable as I created you to be, my beautiful Day Star. A godly temptation if there ever was such a thing." She looked up into the stars above us. "I've simply outdone myself with you." And then she glowed and looked back down at me. "Would you agree?"

"Yes," I said. Even that early in my life I knew the answer to most of the questions my God had, were merely reflective formalities—a mirror for her to gaze upon and revel in her own self-satisfaction.

Our togetherness was barely removed from the sting of sharp fangs, though whose "teeth" dug in deeper was up for debate, when she asked me, "And what have you to report of our fair fallen angel, Lilith? Has my sister's spawn sown the seeds of her mother's monkeys this day?"

I let my head roll limply to the side, so I might look over at Lilith. She slept soundly, though I had no idea how through our howling. "She has informed me that she shall begin creation in the morning."

"Splendid," Life said. And then she reached above her and. . . I had not noticed them before, but shining orbs hung from the limbs above us. Some glowed dark crimson and others a light green. She plucked one of the red ones as quickly and easily as her hand reached to touch it. Reflecting, the fruit simply dropped into her hand as if willed to fall into the very clutches of the hand that would bring its destruction.

My eyes followed the glowing ball as she brought it between us—in front of both of our faces. It emanated understanding even as it approached my face, though I had no knowledge of its name. However, its intrinsic beauty was unmistakable. Round and ripe as the breasts of my mother and as cherry red as the virginity she had taken from me. "What is it?"

"Curious, curious," she said to me, smiling a little as she eyed the orb. "The breath that carried angel's own name is but seconds in your past, and yet you thirst for more knowledge. This is the insatiable appetite for understanding oneself that I've given all beings." She continued to turn the orb in her hand, staring at it as she had stared at me. "*This* is my gift to you, my Son of the Morning. Knowledge and understanding but a snap of your jaws away. And I hold truth of the same in your great God's fist. This is my gift to sister's precious *Purgatory*. Yet you, my most beautiful darling, shall not taste of its wisdom. For I've given you all that you need know. And I shall provide any further understanding that you require to perform your duties successfully."

Believing I understood what she wanted from me, I reached for her hand—the red orb.

Life jerked the freshly plucked prize away from me, and then she held it above her head, against the dark night sky. Outlined only by the twinkling stars, the orb appeared black and had ceased its crimson glow. She smiled down at me. "In the morning," she said softly, "when fair Lilith awakens"—she glanced beside us at Lilith and then back —"you shall offer this gift of knowledge—the light to bring truth to the black of night—to fair sister's daughter." Then she held the orb back in front of me. "And she shall know its sweetness and hold the fruit of understanding in her hands."

I hesitated. I could not stop the question from coming out. "What will become of her?" For Lilith's well-being had slipped its way into my mind and was now spilling its way out of my mouth.

Life frowned, and then she put her smile back in its place. "Come now," she said, "take tribute of tasty treat from my talons before dawn is upon us both. I shall not withhold truth from angel's grasp again."

I placed my hand over hers on the orb. And she quickly clasped her other hand over mine. She spoke into my thoughts: *you shall deliver this to her.* The message pressed into my will.

I held the orb, feeling its cold, crisp roundness. And a foreboding chill swept over my will. Truth fell from my lips even as I tried to stop it. "Yes," I said, "I shall bear fruit to charming and beautiful angel's lips at the dawn. Of this, I shall not fail you."

Life frowned at me again. She moaned—the same wonderful wail that had caressed my ears not moments after my birth. "You misunderstand your mission, Steg," she said, "as the Man-monkey will fumble his great god's *Bible*. This treat isn't destined for my sister's daughter." Then she shook her finger at me slowly as if I *were* the pup that had followed Lilith through the Garden. "And do not be fooled —her charm is deceitful, and her venomous beauty is but vanity. For only a woman who fears her God shall be praised in this way."

Fear. . . I was beginning to understand it.

"Give her the fruit that I bear," she said. "The fruits of her own labor alone shall be her burden in these"—she shook her head in disgust—"gardens of glory. For *this* fruit holds precious and potent seed for Man—only he shall taste of it."

Man, I thought. Even as I had joined with her, my Great Mother's thoughts of the creature Lilith would create spoke misery to my mind.

"He will know all," my Great Mother continued, "and Eden's daughter shall learn quietly with all submissiveness, that her Great Mother . . . is not. For I shall not permit her to teach or exercise authority over Man; rather, she shall remain quiet and calm. Adam shall eat of this *apple* and have knowledge of sin. And then Lilith shall only be saved through bearing his children. And *then* only if she live in faith and love and worship, with self-control toward her one and only God, Life."

I looked up at my Great Mother just as she jerked her head behind her and stared up into the stars at the heavens to be. "How long must I remain?" I asked.

She seemed startled and distracted by something she saw in the stars. Slowly, her attention turned back to me. "Fare well, my serpent," she said. "In seven days this shall all be a fond memory of motherly love. And we will share fruit of sister's Garden together . . . as we have shared each other's fruit on this night."

Then, my Great Mother streaked into the dark night sky and was gone. And the warm blanket of darkness and the twinkle and flicker of the stars above the sap trees were the only witnesses to my sin-soaked hearts.

I held the shining red orb above me. "Apple," I said softly. Then I looked at my slumbering Lilith.

— III —

SHE WAS MY God, and I was her beautiful creation. Who was I to. . .? Understanding her words that night had been as confusing as my new life. She was my . . . love? I was created for that purpose. Of that I was certain. But there was something else—a deep and needful feeling grew inside me, slithering and twisting itself around both of my hearts, pushing out the instincts and instructions I was created to carry out.

I stared at the apple of knowledge, wondering what it might taste like. I held it to my face and breathed in deeply through my nose. Even its smell spoke sin to me. I could have plunged my own teeth into it right then and there. There was no one to stop me. But I didn't . . . and in that decision, tiny as it was, the fate of Man was decided.

Knowledge? I thought. Would it be sweet . . . or sour? Or possibly both? And why would my Great Mother withhold such a wondrous tribute from her sister's child? My confused hearts longed to taste a wisdom that would deliver them from the feelings that only grew stronger.

I rolled toward Lilith, remarkably still motionless next to me. The Garden's soft earth floor barely made mention of my movement.

My Great Mother's morning sun was just making itself known, flickering an orange-fire color into the tops of the sap trees. I shivered and shook, anticipating the impending warmth. I smiled and tucked the apple behind me. Then I gently reached over and touched Lilith's long hair. The light curls in it were smooth and soft between my fingers.

Lilith leapt into the air, jumping to her feet as some sort of wild cat that could spring upon prey in an instant. And I rolled back hard, completely surprised. I felt the apple under my back and I reached to protect it. Then I sat up.

She spun, looking wildly around at the Garden—everywhere but at me. "Unhand precious angel's locks, demon!" she shouted at nothing. "Or I shall separate terrible troll from tasty tail!" She swung her bare back wildly as if her wings were still attached and could be used to slice at an attacker.

She spoke inconceivable things—vile thoughts escaped her lips. *The black has taken—*

She shouted all around her, never looking directly at me, "And with angel's wings I shall take toe and digit from any who dare to—" She felt wildly at her back. Then she did look at me. "Devil!" she screamed as her wild eyes met mine. "What have you done with angel's wonderful wings? They are cropped and flown from my back even as I sleep. Villain!"

"Calm!" I almost shouted. I had no idea what she was saying—I had done nothing. "Angel's own Eden has taken Lilith's wings!" I somehow got to my knees. "They are tribute for task of purpose in her Garden. We spoke of this not one day—"

"Where are. . .?" Lilith said. Then she calmed slightly and began to look around the Garden with a more familiar eye. "This is the Garden . . . of my Great Mother, Eden?"

"In name of the same," I said to her. "We slept not inches apart under warm blanket of darkness only moments ago. And I am *not* demon devil as you speak. I am here to assist you in purpose of creation only. Do you not remember?"

"Liar!" she screamed, and then she rushed at me.

I plowed over backward as Lilith's body slammed into me. And she swung fist and fury at me as if I had robbed her of her own virginity while she slept. "Deceitful snake!" she shouted. "I shall not be fooled by you! Fair Mother warned me of your treachery. And now you have taken my talons from toe and replaced them with—" She continued to swing at me and I held up both of my arms to protect myself and the apple. "You have left angel with marred scar to carry into eternity. It is blasphemy and forbidden by our—"

"What talons have I taken from you?" Her blows struck me about my face, but they didn't bring pain. As far as I remember it, they actually felt pleasurable. I smiled at her and it only made her more angry. "Witness angel's own digits!" I shouted.

"Do not shine serpent's sinful eyes at me!" she screeched. "For I shall split open your stomach and feast on your guts!"

And that revelation was a little more than I was prepared for, because I grabbed both of her arms and held her hard. I had no knowledge of the deeds she accused me of committing. In fact, my hearts had harbored quite the opposite since I awoke in her mother's Garden. "Stop!" I shouted. "I bear no ill-will toward fair creature, be you winged angel or Woman as you are. I am here as your servant alone. Not demon of destruction and death as you hallucinate me to be." And a feeling crept its way from my hands on her wrists, down my arms and into my hearts. To parts of me, it was as familiar as the night before with my God, but now there was more. And I knew she felt it too. Maybe not in herself, but my interest and intentions were a truth to us both.

When she felt them, she tried to pull away. Yet I held her wrists firm. I was surprisingly—to me at the time, anyway—very strong. "Unhand angel's arms!" she shouted. And then she felt them stiffening toward her. "My mother Eden burned at the stake!" she shouted, looking down between us at my waist. "What staffs steel from serpent's own stomach?"

The previous night I had not needed explanation for their shape, size or seductive strength—they had just existed . . . as my creator had wanted I believed. Yet now—then—with Lilith astride me as my Great Mother had been not hours before, I felt . . . shame. "I am sorry," I said. "I know not their hearts' desires, nor how to control them." I looked up at her. "I . . . I only realize my own hearts."

She relaxed a little, but offered one tug of resistance before calming completely. "They are"—she tilted her head, staring at them as they stared back—"mesmerizing," she said. She shifted herself on top of me slightly, tilting her head to the side to look at them both. "*These* are your own desire toward the daughter of Eden's Garden?"

"I am sorry," I said. It was all I could say. I let go of her wrists. "I—why did you scream out at me before? I've not harmed nor hindered you in any way? Do you not dream of your Mother as I do?" I thought it might be better to shift our focus from *them* for the moment, as I realized that my body's parts and purposes were made for my great God, Life's, own purposes. I was not quite certain that they were mine to do with as I pleased. And yet reasoning with them was . . . difficult.

Lilith continued to stare. "I"—she finally looked into my eyes—"I saw you and I saw . . . me, on fire and surrounded by"—she looked around us as if to make certain we were alone—"angels . . . angels with deadly intent of mutiny and murder. And they held me to"—she looked down at her feet and wiggled her toes—"to amputate limb from Lilith's life." Then she looked around us at the Garden again. I could see her confusion slowly withering even as my intentions toward her bloomed from my hearts.

I let go of her wrists, grabbed her by the waist and picked her up and off of me. Then I stood and helped her to her feet.

Lilith seemed dazed by the dawn more than my body. And her dream was keeping her thankfully focused on something besides my. . . What her nightmare had been, at that time. . . The way her eyes bulged as she recounted it spoke of a real danger. But from what I knew of myself, it was simply impossible. "I'd never harm you," I said softly, as I caressed her back to attempt to reassure her of it, "as Woman *or* precious angel in Heaven."

She continued to stare at me, stopping only to glance again at the surrounding forest. "I slept?" she asked.

"Yes," I said, removing my hand from her back. I knew it would be better if I didn't elaborate on the events that occurred as she did. "Quite soundly."

She purposefully didn't look back to my waist, and as her eyes were now softening their stare, it was a good thing. We still had work to do. She hesitated and looked around as if still dragging her mind from its dream. "And my Mother's garden remains. . .?"

"Sinfully silent," I said to her. "As we are in danger of your task falling to the evening again if we do not—"

"Yes," she said, sheepishly. Then she walked away a few feet. She stopped and shook her head. "My all-knowing serpent seems to have allowed me to slumber whilst he slithers himself awake, as if the Garden shall simply"—she threw her hands up into the air—"tend to itself."

I would learn that Lilith—eternities later I would realize that all of her kind—could shift passion and purpose both quickly and crazily. A twisting tongue of desire in one moment and a dagger of damnation in the next. I would also learn that I was no fledgling at that talent myself.

"And yet," I said, "even as I bring gift of Garden's future, I am received by your bittersweet beating?"

She stopped eyeing the rising sun and turned her back toward it to face me. Outlined in the bright orange light, as my great God Mother burned the sun into the misty morning of the Garden, Lilith's hair glowed at the edges. "A gift?" she said, smiling. "From my serpent . . . for me?" She grinned at me as if she had awoken with a smile on her face—no trace that the day had begun with her attacking me.

But staring at her form and beauty began to reverse the effect that we both desperately needed gone—they both stiffened again. I would come to understand that Life had given her serpents single-minded "snakes" of their own. I looked toward where I had left the apple. "Yes, I—"

The undergrowth was thick and heavy, and despite all of the shades of green, accentuated by only occasional branches of brown. And the glowing red apple that Life had entrusted to me . . . was nowhere to be found.

I fell to my knees and ripped into the underbrush, clawing and tearing at branches and shrubs until my hands bled. "Where is it!" *She will not be pleased with this*, I tried to push the thought from my mind.

Lilith stood behind me. "And *now* omniscient snake has lost precious present," she said, "as the time for my own task ticks slowly back toward darkness."

I could feel her staring at me . . . and smell her sweetness. "I placed it here," I spoke down at the dirt. Then I stopped, sat up on my knees and looked back at her. "Until an angry angel decided to—"

As she stood with her arms crossed under her breasts and her hands deep underneath her armpits, Lilith's form was even more powerful. I looked away as fast as my hearts would let me. I looked down at my waist. *They* didn't want to. I stared at the bushes, pretending to go back to looking for my Mother's apple.

Lilith giggled behind me.

"I don't labor for your laughing, waif!" I said, sifting at nothing and staring into the dirt in front of me. "Apple is godly gift for the benefit of Garden's purpose." I moved some branches, going back to the spot where Lilith had been on top of me. I felt sure I had. . .? But the apple was not there.

"How big is it?" Lilith asked behind me, neither of us having known anything of the Garden's fruit a mere night prior to my impending first failure.

"What?"

"How large is precious gift?" Lilith asked. "Large small . . . gigantic?"

I held my fist behind me and shook it a little. "The size of my own *fist*," I said.

"Ah," she muttered behind me. I could feel her enjoying my rising frustration and panic. "So, not formidable at all? . . . I realize how one might *misplace* such a small thing, even a saintly serpent such as yourself."

"Please," I said, hoping my voice's tone alone would be enough to stop her from taunting me. I moved another branch only to find more green growth and brown earth. *You are failing her. . .* my mind heckled the thought at me, not doing justice to the magnitude of my Great Mother's more than likely reaction.

"Please?" Lilith said behind me. "Help you? Is it not *you* who has been sent to help me?"

The pause gave me hope that she had finally run dry of fuel to pour on my fire.

Maddeningly, she had not—her heckling continued. "Shall my second day in the Garden be spent assisting my own advisor, while the task of Man lies mired in the morning, quickly turning to the miserable middle of the hot day?

"The fruit of time slips from my grasp, snake, even as your precious . . . 'apple' did you say? It seems your fruit has found its way from your grasp. I may have to inform my Great Mother to summon second serpent from her sister."

I believe I grumbled behind me at her. Though it could have been a grunt, as all my thoughts had turned to an unexplainable panic at the possibility that I had lost my Mother's gift. I was discovering all manner of sound and sinful thoughts as I rushed for its recovery.

"Tell me, great Day Star," Lilith said, "is your apple round?"

I wasn't sure if she actually thought she was assisting me, or if she was making sport of my plight. Either way, her voice, which had moments before given me mind for marrying with her body, was now making me miserable.

I crawled on my hands and knees, ducking under a shrub to avoid being cut. It was filled with sharpness, and sliced into my face and sides as I frantically searched. "Yes, yes," I growled back at her, "it is surely as round as——" I tried not to think about them, but seeing Lilith's arms crossed in front of her had only made their effect on my "companions" worse. And just then, a thought spiked its way into my mind. *What will she do to me if I don't find it?*

"How round is it?" Lilith said, annoyingly unconcerned.

"It is as round as the sun behind you," I replied, and then I raised my voice, "and twice as raging red!"

"That is *very* red," I barely heard her say. "I wonder, does it glow?" she asked. "It would be helpful to task of recovery if Garden's gift shined brighter than the darkness of fallen angel's current shelter under shrubbery."

She made a compelling case—the fruit my Mother had entrusted to me *did* glow. I would have surely found it in the dark of the under-growth of—I stopped cold and hung my head, knowing but not wanting to ask. "Eden's daughter holds the apple . . . even as her serpent slices and slams at the very ground of the Garden"—I closed my eyes—"does she not?"

Her voice was playful and once again sweet in my ears. "She does."

I stood up slowly, rising through the dense and dark underbrush of Lilith's entrusted Garden, not to mention my mind's confusion. I gazed through the clear and concise understanding that who I had thought was a simple servant of her own God, was actually a form and force to invoke the feelings I had for my own.

This Woman who would create Man had now moved from my terrible task of spy . . . to a growing sentiment for sin. And that was the first time my mind realized the truth of what that sin might bring. *Life will kill you.* But that thought would not be heard through the need in my hearts.

Lilith held the big red apple barely a beautiful breath from her mouth. "So this is Day Star's godly gift to console my own lost wings? Celebrate the day of the dawn of Man?"

As I stepped from the bushes, Lilith eyed the apple in her hand. I felt cuts over my entire body. Some ran as red as the apple and others bled nothing but black. Then I ignored them all and focused on Lilith's mouth next to the apple. I could not allow her to bite it.

But neither could I let her understand how important it was to me for her not to. I felt that deeply. For though my Great Mother could seemingly read my thoughts, I didn't need to read Lilith's—her eyes spoke of a pondering mind of mischief.

I started with the truth I knew. She would have smelled anything else as deception. "It is a delicacy of multiplying fruit, yes"—I pointed at the green and red apples above us, hanging low and waiting to be plucked—"but this particular one bears knowledge of that same task. To be sure it is a round red raven, cawing to be consumed. And it *does* share task of Woman's own duty."

Lilith moved the apple closer to her mouth. "Then it is only fitting," she said, "that Woman share task *and* knowledge of raven's fruit." She opened her mouth.

I ran toward her. "No!"

She jerked the apple behind her as my own Mother had. "No?" she said. "Who are you, *advisor*, to tell guardian of the Garden 'no'?"

"Please," I said, "you cannot eat it. It . . . it isn't meant for you!"

Lilith lowered the apple. She looked around the Garden. The light of day raced on around us, and she had yet to fulfill its purpose. "Yet sinful serpent and saintly Mother of Man are the only beings here, so who, pray tell, could the fruit of my Mother Eden's womb be meant for, I wonder?"

"You are aware," I said. And I felt the words of my Mother's mind as if they were my own. "Knowledge and knowing are for Woman's spawn. *Man* must eat the apple, lest Woman be—"

"Be what?"

Somehow I knew the answer to all of her questions—any that she might ask. My great God, Life, had shared more with me than I had imagined when we coupled. But I didn't believe that Lilith would appreciate that revelation . . . nor any other that I might share regarding the fate of Woman throughout the eternities. Certainly not as it pertained to my Mother's Word in her own *Bible*.

"Be what?" Lilith repeated her question, cocking her hips to the side, placing her elbow on her waist and showing me the "apple" of my own hearts as she did. "If you are here to assist me, snake, slither twisted tongue from mouth and speak."

I don't know how, and I don't know why I thought of it, but being called a snake certainly may have provided the idea. What delivered the message didn't feel like either of my own hearts. "It is *poison*," I said, "for you." It was the only thing I could think of that would stop her from biting into it.

Lilith almost dropped the apple. "What?"—she stared down at it as if it would rush at her—"Why would you give me such a thing? You treacherous—"

"For you," I raised my voice to stop hers. "For precious daughter it is most certainly poison, and will take your mortal life," I said. I paused, struggling for the reasoning to back up my claim. "*But* . . . for the seed you must sow . . . this apple is simply knowing and . . . and truth." And then the lies became easier. "For every apple in this Garden contains this as its fruit. And when we find yours, it shall be no different." I hoped—I think it was the very first time that I prayed to the stars—that my explanation would be enough.

— IV —

I PRAISED THE impending stars that my explanation worked. And that was how all little white lies and the entire phenomena of lying to obtain a desired result began. Unable and unwilling to deal with the consequences of truth, the alternative became something that staved off the discomfort of the present . . . only to ensure its replacement by the absolute misery of the truth of the future.

And like a cancer that is free to run rampant as long as it is hidden from the bright light of discovery, lies simply get bigger, more malignant, until they eventually . . . kill you.

Yet what I only thought I knew of truth and lies was nothing compared to the deceit and misery that would befall Lilith and me in our not-so-distant future.

"What is it?" I asked, staring down at Lilith's wild creation. For upon retrieving my Mother's apple, she had reprimanded me briefly and then set herself to her task.

She had plucked a single strand of golden hair from her head, and then buried it in the moist earth beside one of the Garden's many crystalline babbling brooks. Then we both retreated to the shore and soaked our feet in the warm waters. Then we waited, laughing and smiling at Lilith's taunting of me and my "precious" apple.

After a while, though time with Lilith had a way of passing too quickly, we heard a shrieking sound and then raging shouts and screams from where she had buried her hair. Fearing for her safety, I had steeled myself to perform my duties of security as her sole protector. I could not. . . I would not allow harm to come to her. That was my truth at the time.

The creature—spawned from Lilith's own hair—was more monkey than the man I had imagined. It stood up from the dirt, snarling and spitting as it seemed to grow out of the ground. And the hair. . . When it finally shook all the dust and dirt it could from its mangy scalp and body, it faced only Lilith.

I was quite shocked by my feelings when it spoke. "Who are you?" he asked.

It was most certainly a *he*, though a more hideous male of any species I've yet to see since. However, as you may have already guessed, my judgment at the time was . . . clouded at best.

Lilith seemed without concern. I had many. The greatest of which was the creature's hair-covered snake and the erroneous eggs beneath it —the purpose of which I found my face turning red in anger at the thought.

When Lilith spoke, she sounded more benevolent than she had with me. "I am Lilith, daughter of the great Eden," she said to him. Then she motioned her arms around the three of us—I was beginning to feel like three was one too many. "Eden is the Great Mother of all you see before you—nature herself."

It was as grand and as simple an explanation as a creature who had just been birthed from the black nothingness could get. I found myself wishing Life would have given me as simple a revelation upon my own birth.

"Lilith?" it said, grunting as I would come to know pigs. Then it pointed its disgusting finger at me.

I had the urge to reach out and rip it from the monkey's hand, but held fast, trying to remember my purpose. However, if it had offered up any movement at all towards Lilith, I believe I might have done worse than that.

"And *what* is this?" the Man-monkey asked, still not even showing me the respect of addressing me directly.

"*What?*" I thought to myself. "I am not what," I said to it. And then my mouth simply spit out the words. "I am Day Star, Son of the Morning, mortal man," I said. "I am the. . ." I really had no idea how to describe my relationship to Life at that point. It wasn't so much that I felt shame or guilt over my Great Mother and my love for her; it was more that those feelings lay elsewhere as well. I looked at Lilith briefly, then back at the man-*thing*. "I am the son of the great God, Life, the bringer of light and truth to all *beasts* and beings, including yourself. And I shall thank you to address me directly as such."

I could feel Lilith's discomfort at my words. She fidgeted next to me. "I believe what fair fallen angel, Steg, is saying"—I had no idea that she knew my name . . . or how, but it fell from her lips like nectar to my ears—"is that he is here as my personal advisor and confidant. It's his duty to assist me in ushering in the very first eternity of creation." She looked at me and smiled and I half-smiled back. "It is a very important responsibility."

I would find that *Man* was a creature of few and flavorless words. "Then *what* am I?" It asked, looking around as if there was some better world to have been birthed into. "What is my purpose here . . . in this place?"

It was a question I had secretly but naively hoped to never hear asked. And I didn't want to know why I felt that way, but in the truth between us . . . I did. And that *is* the truth about lies—the ones you tell yourself are the worst.

"Your purpose," I said it before I weighed the consequences, "is to understand and protect and to behave as she commands you—"

"What is my name?" it asked Lilith. Not even the courtesy to let me finish my—"Who are you to me?"

The Man-monkey was maddening, but before I could tend defense or obtain satisfaction from the creature's slight, Lilith said it, "I am your wife."

Adam. . . It was a disgusting name in my mind and I . . . I *hated* it, was the feeling in both of my hearts—I hated him. And that fire of hate was foreign to me, yet something knew how to stoke its flames, for it would do nothing from there but grow.

I sat underneath the sap trees and listened to the cicadas attempt to *chirr* the three of us to sleep. Though there would be at least one godly offspring that would not go quietly into the black of my Great Mother's second night over the Garden.

I stared at my hand and the red apple in it—the task and fate that Life dealt me the night before. Lilith had been focused enough on her own task of birthing Adam into being, that she failed to even ask about giving the apple to him. I tried not to imagine them basking in the darkness of the garden, as Life and I had the night before.

I turned the glowing red orb in my hand. *Apple*, I thought. *Ultimate knowledge and understanding—truth.* . . How could I give it to that *thing?* . . . *I will not!*

In less than a day the creature had taken away all hope of obtaining what my hearts had only begun to long for. And now both of those beating beasts knew . . . I would give Adam nothing else.

That night, I carried the apple as far away and for as long as I dared leave Lilith alone with Adam. Just far enough that I would be able to conceal the fruit's location without leaving Lilith unprotected from its intended jaws of destruction.

I dug with rocks and sticks until my bare hands bled. Black and red blood flowed worse than the cuts and scrapes I had earned trying to recover the apple that morning.

Far from Lilith's understanding of why, and hidden from whatever Life's knowledge and wisdom would allow this dirty man-creature to possess, and deep down beneath my slowly breaking hearts, I buried Adam's precious apple. This time . . . no one would find it.

And that was the biggest lie I ever told myself.

— V —

EXHAUSTED FROM DIGGING, I fell asleep by the very brook where Lilith and I had waited for Adam to grime his way into the Garden—infect himself into our beautiful sanctuary.

I had barely arrived at a heaven I now longed for. And before the possibilities of my new life could be fully explored, those wonderful thoughts of my future in the Garden slowly turned to the acid of a knowledge that I wanted nothing more than to leave the putrid place and never return.

Why am I here? It was the last thought I remembered before falling asleep. For if it was simply to assist Lilith in tending to Adam in her Mother's Garden, a more heinous hell I could not imagine. Anywhere . . . anything would be better than that!

Life and dream intertwined that night and my Great Mother, God, appeared to me again, shining and smiling her warmth down upon my chest. I was thankful for her, though silently wished her to be . . . someone else. "Do mine eyes deceive," she moaned, "or does precious fallen Day Star, Steg, slumber miles from man and mate? Has my serpent lost his stomach for surveillance so soon? Or perhaps you simply wished for more . . . privacy upon your God's second visitation to my now victorious virgin's bosom?"

And I realized the question was imminent, yet I prayed to the rock I had buried the apple under that it was not.

Life smiled at me as she hovered. Then she floated down and

landed across my waist. "Tell me," she said, as we each entered the other's body, "does Adam's belly boil and burn from digestion of fruit? Has apple pumped its poisonous purpose into precious Eden's prized piglet's mate?"

We were of a similar mind on Adam being a filthy swine of a Man-monkey, however the discussion of it was doing nothing to stiffen my . . . resolve.

Life paused and looked into me, most likely feeling the hesitation in my snakes. There would be no hiding it. She flapped her wings wildly and lifted off of me in anger. And the babbling brook and the grove of trees that hung over it, lit up to a spike of bright white light. "You did what?" she shouted. "This isn't the purpose of godly gift. Where have you buried it? Tell me immediately!"

I winced as her mind tried to enter the depths of mine. I had to keep her out. Whatever knowledge my God's apple would give Adam, I wanted him to have nothing. "Nothing!" I shouted back. "He shall have nothing!"

Life slowly fluttered her wings and herself down to a calmer color than white light. Her black eyes grew bigger with the understanding she had seen in my mind. "Ohh," she said, "you . . . *hate* him." She eyed me curiously and then smiled. "How interesting that is."

I turned my face slightly away from her still-dimming light. And almost sensing it, at that same time she turned herself down to a low glow, just enough that I could still see her eyes.

She landed next to me, laid down and then slumped into my chest. Her wings folded back behind her and she slipped her first finger's talon out to its full length. Then she drew the spiking sharp tip of it across my bare chest, not quite slicing my skin as she scratched a twisting "S" toward my waist. "And yet what is hate, fair fallen angel, but another name for love never to be tasted . . . before it is lost forever?"

I turned my head away slightly.

"Of this I've warned you," she said. "You shall learn to let sleeping dogs lie where they must, lest they dig through the depths of your hearts, leaving them only suitable for burying the bones of your past."

By the time her sharp talon arrived at my snakes, the pair of them were hissing and striking at it, steeled and stiffened as was Life's purpose in the first place.

When she was finished with me, my Great Mother stood and assisted me to my feet. She shook her wings and waist feathers dry and then stared at my face.

It was an ancient gaze. One of understanding and patience—a passionate mother, but a forgiving teacher as well. Or so I believed at the time. "I suppose," she spoke even as her wings began to hum, preparing for her flight back to. . . I really had no recollection of the place she would return to other than the blackness of my short-lived birth.

I had been created—born to life and sprouted wings as an angel—and quicker than that I had lost them both and been plunged into a purgatory of my creator's prideful plot. Yet I would have had it no other way, for as long as Lilith remained the Garden's caretaker, I would walk it as her serpent . . . slave if I had to.

"I suppose," Life said again, "that as long as we find ourselves at the crossroads of creation . . . my love"—she fluttered above me, smiling —"we shall simply have to make the best of a difficult dilemma. For

Life always finds a way, does she not?"

I looked up at her, confused at her allowing me to defy her in any way.

I wasn't sure if she was talking to me or herself at the end, but the next thing she said, I knew was meant for my ears. "However, I wonder what precious Eden's daughter might think . . . were she to ever find out that saintly Day Star she considers confidant, is only 'venomous virgin' . . . by half?"

It was the first time I had known a threat—felt the venom of impending vengeance upon my ears before tasting its effects in my flesh and feathers. But having delivered my own venom into Life, not once but twice, there was no ounce of lie in my God's words. She would destroy me if she had to—a means to an end I didn't yet see.

My Great Mother had marked me for her eternity and I was to be a slave for it, chained so by my own desire for Lilith. Life was no longer the benevolent master I had met when I opened my eyes for the first time. Now, my eyes wide and begging, the master I would have gladly served to my death . . . had silently slipped from my grasp and into the grimy grip of another God's cruel creation, Adam. *Adam and Eden*, the thought slipped through my mind like sand through fingers.

"Tomorrow, precious snake," Life said to me just before she left, "you shall resurrect the fruit that I gave you and deliver it to task. And we shall speak no more of this 'love' you languish in for Lilith. Life is your loving Mother and only lover, my lovely angel. In time you shall understand and accept this . . . as all my children eventually do."

Many eternities later, I would realize that those who casually bantered and batted the word "love" around with such frequency . . . had no concept of its merit or meaning. I watched as my "love" flew up into the stars and disappeared, leaving me to my hell.

Shortly after Life left, I heard a great howling sound. It grew louder, echoing its way through the Garden. My face went slack and blankness filled me at first. But then I closed my eyes and clenched my fists.

Short of cicada, I had neither seen nor heard any other fauna produced in Lilith's short time. . . I really had no idea how long she had been in the Garden, but I had seen no other creature capable of such a ruckus.

The howling grew louder, and I ground my teeth together, gritting them back and forth. I could bear the assault on my ears no longer!

I raced from the far side of the glen—the farthest we had explored in our short stay. Brush clipped my legs, and my shoulders bounced and banged off of trees as I ran. Barely taking breath, I willed my way through the dark towards what I only wished was the unknown.

As I got closer, the howling turned to moaning, and I could not deny the truth of it. But my mind still wanted to deceive my hearts. I would learn soon enough what my hypocrisy had wrought upon my head.

As I burst into the clearing, I came face to face with Lilith, deep in the throes of what pains me to remember. She stared through me, seemingly oblivious that I was even there. She was not, however, oblivious to Adam.

On impulse I grabbed her by her shoulders and picked her up off of him as I ran past them both. Then I stood her up by a tree—she was still lost in it—and I turned back toward Adam to deliver a taste of my own misery.

SMACK! My face lit up with fire and stars shot through my eyes, and then my ribs took what felt like a foot right through them and I heard one of them crack and I yelled out in pain, "Ahh!" Then I fell to the ground and coughed blood and that sent sharp shards of spiking misery into my surely broken ribcage.

I slumped onto my back and the last thing I saw or heard was Adam over my face, "Your snake has lost his way in the dark of his Mother's night, wife." And his fist came down fast. "I shall help him recover it!" Pain slammed into my face as hard as Adam's claim of "wife" hammered my hearts.

SMACK! A bright white light split into my mind. Almost thankfully, I went to the soothing comfort of the nothingness—the black. Far from the Man-monkey . . . and my Lilith's lost flower.

LOVE

— VI —

I WOKE STARING up at an angel. At least that's what sunshine in the garden, Lilith's warm smile radiating down at me and the sounds of something chirping felt like.

I touched my chin and then worked my jaw. The pain hardly compared to the spiking misery in my ribs every time I tried to take a deeper breath than a small sniff. But none of it compared to the heavy burden in my hearts.

"What gives you right, serpent?" my assailant's voice shouted from behind Lilith.

I was thankful I could not see him, but I turned my head away from his voice anyway. The Garden had grown green, greener than our first day in it for certain. It was now more jungle than forest since I slipped into the black and came back.

Lilith turned and spoke behind her, "You've beaten him, husband," she said. The words were worse than any pain that I felt. "Now, let him rest and recuperate to purpose of the Garden." She turned back and looked down at me again.

I dared not look at her, but she grasped my face and gently turned my head even as a single tear escaped my eye. I silently wished to never see them as I had, and would have gladly welcomed my eye be popped out rather than shed one more tear over that memory. Lilith cocked her head slightly, gave me a comforting smile, and then she reached down and touched my broken rib.

I tightened and moaned and winced up at her. Yet her hand felt. . . I looked at her body, truly "seeing" it for the first time. And I knew she was—we were *all* naked. Something flew past and I looked up at it. Then more of them . . . and more and more and the cheeping squeaked into the silence of the morning. My eyes followed one of the little red thrushes until it lit on a branch.

Lilith wiped the trail of the tear from my cheek. "Do you like them?" she asked, looking back up. "I made them yesterday."

"You've made miniature. . ." I said, but I was confused as we had barely birthed her monkey, Adam. "Yesterday? . . . What day is this?"

"You have slept through one glorious day of creation in my Mother's Garden, Steg," Lilith said. "I feared you—let us pray to Eden that you remain awake for the next four."

I looked back toward the small flying angels. "How many of them are—" But pain seared into my side and I had to stop talking. I winced and tried to forget the miserable monkey that I knew lurked behind Lilith. I watched the little flying angels rush past. "How many days do we have?" I asked.

"Oh, precious Sage," she said softly, "there are seven . . . seven days of creation. Has your great *Mother* not told you of this? Of the consequences should we fail?"

I ignored her and looked at the small flying creatures. "What do you call them?" I asked, longing only for my own wings to return and fly me away from the ungodly Garden of Eden. "And . . . why do they sing?"

"They are birds, fair serpent," she said, "and they sing simply because they are free to do so. Tomorrow, Eden willing, my Mother and I shall bring forth the rest of the earth for them to soar over." She looked up as a few more of them flew by. "Were it this easy with *all* creatures in our garden." She looked back at me. "Might I. . . What on my Mother's green Earth were you trying to accomplish, Steg? I am set to task of purpose. Seeds must be sown. This is the Word of both our gods. The Garden must flourish and Woman shall bear fruit and multiply. So wife shall lie with her husband. Which leads me to —"

I turned my head away.

Lilith reached to my chin and through my protests over my aching jaw, she gently pulled my face back to look at hers again. "Steg, where is Adam's apple?" She had not forgotten.

Knowledge and understanding. . . I mulled the thought over in my mind as Lilith stood up and walked a few feet away, toward him. So far, the more knowledge I gained about the new world I was created into. . . The more I understood of my Great Mother's life on Earth, the more miserable, frustrated and saddened I became.

If knowledge and understanding and truth brought that, then I reasoned that maybe it would not be such a terrible idea to give Adam his *precious* apple. Shove knowledge right down his monkey throat— let *him* choke on the bitter ash of "understanding" for a change! *Yes*, I thought, *that is exactly what I shall do.*

I coughed a little laugh, but steel rage twisted into my side. I held onto the pain for an instant, letting it sear into my mind. I would use that pain to my own purposes soon enough.

Lilith, hearing my discomfort, knelt back beside me. "Shh," she spoke softly, running her hand through my hair. "You must calm yourself. Your anger and tears shall serve no purpose."

"Lilith," I said. "My God has said, 'You must not eat fruit from any tree in the garden.' I am curious, what has your Great Mother, Eden, decreed of her own Garden's fruit?"

Lilith thought for a moment. "She simply said that we must not eat the fruit from the tree in the *middle* of the Garden. Do not even touch it. For if we do, we shall die."

I would know and make friends with the fact that all lies are easily concealed . . . if veiled under threat of death.

— VII —

"LEAVE HIM," ADAM'S voice turned the warmth in my hearts from Lilith's gaze to an icy blanket of cold indifference. "If we truly have but seven days, I've not time nor inclination to teach your snake to interrupt marital felicity with my fist. Your Great Mother has barely created the sky above and task, as you've explained it, falls dangerously —"

"That's enough," Lilith said in a voice that I was coming to know. "We need this serpent for saintly service as much as we need flailing from my husband's fist. I swear to my Mother's Garden, between serpent and Man, I know not which of you is worse." She continued, now muttering questions only to herself as she spoke, "Eden help me, one of you animals is sure to be the death of us all. How my Great Mother believes that *this* is the way of Genesis? . . . Eh, the both of you, cease sinful seditions lest the sun shine on Sunday and we all turn to bitter *ash*."

I was content to let Lilith defend me, but that word—"husband"— cut into me each time she spoke it. Yet her defense was the least painful part of my third day in the Garden thus far. Though, the Man-*pig* was correct—I was wont to admit—seven days was the mandate and we were burning into the third one with our . . . "disagreement" over how we should all proceed. Which was to say nothing of my mistaken belief that Lilith's warning was mere frustration.

I decided to change my approach. "We may yet find success in this day," I said, "buried beneath concern for precious Woman's welfare."

"You buried it?" Lilith said. I would also learn that she could ferret out the truth of things, be they veiled or not. "Why would you—where is it?" And once set to a purpose, she was single-minded in her approach. It was a beautiful truth. "You shall take us there"—she cocked her head and looked at me sternly, nodding as if to force my own head to do the same—"*now*."

I smiled back. I leaned and tried to look behind her, but could see nothing of the monkey, Adam. "I thought it wise to protect precious apple," I told her, "from the mangy mouth of your Man-monkey maggot. Until we discerned his disposition for destruction." I felt my jaw. "I don't think it was an unwise decision, given recent . . . events. Are you sure that he is domesticated enough to—"

"Get up," Lilith said. She stood up, grabbing my hand as she did.

As she pulled at me—though it felt more like jerking and yanking at the time—my ribs screamed the rage of a sharp spear at my side, and when I winced at the pain that it sent, my jaw sent fresh hurt into my head. I groaned. "Careful," I said, staggering slightly. "My memory may be blighted by rough handling from fallen angel's own hand. And then where would a miserable Man-monkey's *understanding* be? Precious apple lost to amnesia from yet another *battering* of my brains."

I looked at Adam, now fully visible and sitting on a large rock with the ragged end of some sort of weed, swirling and swaying in his mouth. As he chewed it like cows would come to chew their own cud, I only glanced. . . I didn't want to think of it, much less see it, but his own "serpent" was disgustingly docile. I raged at the reason.

I spit blood at the ground in front of me. Just enough in Adam's direction to cause Lilith to grab my upper arm. If that was what it took, I knew I would expend a thousand—ten billion—vials of my venom toward Man to have her hold me like that.

Adam pulled the plant from his greedy teeth. "Slither yourself sane, serpent," he said, "so we may set ourselves back to task of retrieving raven's robbed fruit. For if dawn comes on the Sabbath before our success, I shall give snake a renewed reason to shine his hateful eyes upon me forever."

I smiled back at him through the pain in my jaw. It would take no more from him to accomplish *that* feat.

— VIII —

THE GREAT GOD, Eden, fluttered deep inside the blackness, high above her Garden, watching. She was heartened at the prospects and promise that it held. Life would flourish there and she would mother it to its glory. A fact that she would tend to *personally* if need be. This she felt with a certainty more deeply than the knowledge that her jealous sister would try to prevent it. It left only to Lilith. . . She could not risk her sister thwarting creation.

Eden had known to play the nattering nabob of naiveté, never revealing cunning nor cause for concern to her vain, yet dangerously powerful sister. Eden needed Life for her light, but once the Garden was filled with birthing earth, Life would have no use for her—she would strike with as much venom as she birthed her snakes to inject into her own. . . Her sister had become seductive and sinful and it disgusted her.

There was little doubt as to why Life would strike, but the how? How would her own sister attempt to thwart anything that would rival her own glory and beauty and endless existence? For once Eden's creations were ready, they would be allowed the fruit of everlasting being—the apples that grew in the deepest reaches of the Garden. Once earned, Woman and her Man would take their place next to Eden and Life as equals—gods themselves in their own eternity. Together they would all bring precious life to the eternities to come.

Eden watched from the heavens as Life handed the seed of her own children's destruction to her sinister snake—the precious apple of. . . Eden frowned and shook her head slowly. She had hoped against hope that her sister would not lead them down this pathway. Yet something in her knew that their confrontation was inevitable. For were a serpent to. . . She dared not think of the consequences.

It was bad enough that Life had created her servant serpents to slither and share poison with *her*, penetrating and pulsing with them as the mirrors to her own vanity. Now, it was clear that in addition to that dreadful duty, Life planned to use her snakes as vicious vials of venom, destined to deliver their destruction to Eden's own offspring.

This, she could not let happen!

— IX —

I LED LILITH and her hateful *husband,* Adam, through the Garden to the spot where I had buried the apple. I was sure the knowledge it contained would take his anger and hatred and turn it inward upon his own soul. I was actually excited at the prospect of it. Rid myself of the brutal bane of my brief but happy existence in the Garden . . . once and for all the coming eternities.

The brook babbled and the birds sang and my Great Mother began to set the sun. Golden streaks shined through the branches and the fuzzy seeds of the sap trees floated down through its glow. I smiled at the glory of it despite my growing hatred at being there. Ironies were like lies to themselves—the glory of the Garden would not suffer its own condemnation. Every living thing burst with the tenacity of impending propagation. Life would find a way through all of this. She had told me as much.

Yet being there in the middle of it all, I could only think of how the children of Man would come into being and the vile violation that Lilith would have to endure to ensure it. All thought of it pained me beyond what you can imagine. I looked at Adam and could not contain myself—I squinted and shined a snake's eyes back at him.

Adam smiled back with a face and feeling that after five eternities spent dealing with his kind, I can tell you definitively, was nothing less than thoughts of pure mischievous mayhem and murder. "Wipe the grin from your face," he said, "and give location of fruit before your ungodly creator blankets us in her darkness. For when it sets, I shall be forced to warm myself inside the womb of Eden's daughter again . . . until we may retrieve this *apple* under light of the dawn."

The smile left my face and my mind only searched for the pathway to choking Adam's throat. Blasphemy against my Great Mother, God, was one thing, but a threat to Lilith?

Adam turned toward her. Lilith was busy searching all around the spot where I had buried the apple, but I had hidden it well. "Your serpent deceives us, wife, and the sun is setting," Adam said to her. "If he does not divulge its location shortly, I shall part brains from his skull."

Lilith kept searching. More than once, she had stepped right over the rock I put on top of the hole. "I beg of you, bring no such harm to him," she said. Then she stopped and looked at me.

I grinned, overflowing with the guilt of it. And I tried hard not to look behind her at the rock tombstone over the grave of Adam's apple.

But as I've told you, Lilith had a way with her own wisdom. "Steg," she said, "have we repeated my own game? Is it now *you* who hides desired prize behind *daughter's* own back?" She crossed her arms under her breasts again. It was something I could barely tolerate, and I think . . . I think she knew that. "You realize it was jest and I would not. . . I would never . . . unless you advised—" She stopped herself, realizing by my growing smile that she was right.

I shrugged my shoulders sheepishly, silently sharing the memory with her while allowing Adam to feel my satisfaction over knowing the truth of it.

"What?" Adam was bewildered, as he had been thankfully only an impending storm during Lilith's and my first morning in the Garden.

He looked at her smiling at me, and then at me smirking back. "What has serpent and sacred wife done?"

"It was simple wages of a game, husband," Lilith said to him, continuing her smirk at me. "Wages that it seems my serpent will now obtain his pound of flesh to recover. I believe he merely waits for opportune moment to spring the fruit from its hiding place."

I enjoyed watching Adam's face flatten beneath the weight of his own imagination. He most surely wondered what other "games" his *wife* and I might have played. For the same look on his face, I recognized as my own when I tried not to think of him and Lilith on that night.

My face went as slack as his as I tried to understand why my God had done this to me. Why had she created me to divine purpose of creation and then left hearts of sorrow bleeding inside my chest? I prayed to the black of night and Lilith's safety in it, that my Great Mother would rip those hearts out and spare me their ever-growing ache. And I vowed that I would pray to any god that would grant me such a wish.

There was no way I could endure four more days watching Lilith and the beast run rampant through the Garden, much less listen to her nightly moans of—I clenched my jaw and pushed through the thought, concealing it as best I could. Yet that is a lie that anyone who has tried will tell you is impossible to hide.

Adam tilted his head slightly. Then his eyebrows lifted and he stared back at me. "Even now your snake plots inside his mind as he pines away for wifely Woman," he said. Then he turned to Lilith. "Can you not see it?" He turned back to me. "It is written on his—a blind man could tell."

Lilith, despite her knowing, or maybe because of it. . . I will never know. But for some reason, she let that dirty dog of deception lie in the dirt beneath our feet. "Nonsense, husband," she said, almost as if to secretly tell me that it was not the time, "Steg simply repays for my jest." Her eyebrows spoke to me of something else in her words. "Is this not so . . . servant of Life?" Now I could see that her eyes begged me to lie.

What was it? What had I missed in the day I lost to the black? I stared at her, trying to find the truth in her eyes.

Lilith barely moved her head to each side. So small a gesture that I thought it to be nothing. But my hearts knew better. Something *had* happened while I was unconscious, something bad. And the look in Lilith's eyes told me it was probably worse than what I could imagine.

I shrugged my shoulders and tentatively smiled at Adam. "Eh," I said, "it is a debt more easily paid than I imagined. And I grow weary of collecting the interest for it." I walked to the rock not two feet behind Lilith's own. And I shoved it with my foot.

The rock rolled over and down the small embankment, splashing into the brook as we all watched it. Had I more courage at the time, I would have picked it up and stoned Adam's teeth out with it.

As the rock joined hundreds of its hard and heavy brothers and sisters, the current rushed over it, washing it clean and removing all sign that it had once been covered in the deceit of dirt. Such was water—exactly the same as time.

The freshly dug hole and pile of dirt waited with the three of us, listening to the babbling of the brook beside it. The sweet and sooth-ing sounds of water flowing over and around rocks were only interrupted by the smacking sounds of Adam's fists as he beat my face.

He sat on my chest, pinning me to the ground as he pounded his fists at my head. Lilith screamed behind him, begging him to stop.

"Where is it?" Adam shouted as he swung. "Miserable snake, where have you hidden it?"

My arms flailed, struggling to keep up with his fists in order to defend my face. Thankfully, they were keeping the blows from pitching me back to the black. "I don't—" A fist slammed into my jaw and sent my head twisting to the side and blood spurting from my lips.

I had no idea what the answer was, because once Adam removed all the dirt from the hole I had dug—I drew the line at digging it up for him—or maybe Adam just lost patience and clawed into it himself before I had the chance. . . But once he was through digging, we all stared into the empty hole with equal amazement. The fruit—Adam's apple—was not there.

Believing I had made a fool of him—a feat that needed no assistance from me—he set himself to repeating the beating he gave me not two nights before.

Adam backhanded me with his fist and my head swung to the other side and more blood flew from my mouth. I watched the crimson droplets arc in slow motion away from me and land in the pile of dirt we had removed from the apple's supposed hiding place. The blood quickly turned black, mixing with the dirt to form dark miserable mud.

"Does snake take me for a fool?" Adam said. And another blow—I could no longer separate them from each other—whipped my face back.

"It was"—I covered my face as the pounding continued—"it was there!" I tried to shout, but my will was leaving me. "I know it was there," I muttered.

It was the truth.

In retrospect, I know that he—Adam, the father of Man—was simply doing what had to be done. Eden's life was finding a way. Because if my time in the eternities of Life has taught me anything. . . If you require the simple truth from a person's seditious soul, sometimes the most efficient and expedient way is to skip the deception, and merely beat the living Hell out of them.

It isn't as eloquent as I like things nowadays, but the results are undeniably . . . accurate.

"He does not know!" Lilith shouted from somewhere I couldn't see.

My eyes swelled and my vision blurred.

The beating stopped for an instant, and then Adam was off of me. I heard Lilith yell, "No!" And then a loud *SMACK!* And that was the last thing she said before Adam was back on top of my chest.

"Were it not for finding lost fruit, snake," he said, "and the fact that I shall take what you only dream about from Eden's precious daughter while she rests"—spittle sprayed down upon my face as he spoke at me—"I should choke the life from you until your twisted tongue hangs limp from your mouth." He paused and wiped his brow. At least that's what it looked like through my blurred vision. "Now, I shall ask you once more—where is the apple?"

As much as I wanted to tell nothing but lies to the filthy Man-monkey beast. . . I wanted to *kill* him for whatever he had done to silence Lilith. Now he claimed he would. . . My hearts and my head had nothing but truth left as resistance. "I have no"—barely able to spit, I slobbered black blood from my right heart—"earthly idea." I closed my eyes, knowing what was next.

A blinding white light felt like it split my skull, and then I went back to my beautiful black.

— X —

THIS TIME, I awoke alone. The Garden was silent. The night stretched out as black as the nothingness I had been sent back to. I stared up at the stars, through the sap tree branches above me. They leaned and loomed like vultures waiting for me to finally expire, so they could pick my carcass clean. Though any nourishment I might have had as a flesh and feathered angel was now only a bare-boned corpse of cowardice.

I raged at my lack of courage to save Lilith. I would not—this could not be how her life would begin. How it might end.

I was thoroughly beaten . . . but I was not through. I could not be.

"Lilith," I struggled to say it. Even if she would have been there to hear me, I doubt that she could have—my voice barely made sound. But there was no one, and the Garden returned only silence.

I spit out some blood. Which color it was? Even if I could have seen clearly through a swollen eye and fogged mind, I would not have been able to tell in the night. But whichever heart it flowed from . . . had turned stone cold black.

Wincing and grunting through the pain, I pried my eye open. It hurt badly, but I needed to see to find out where he had taken—

Something screeched through the stillness and then a horrible scream and then silence answered it. It was a shrill cry like none I've ever heard since. A cold shiver worked its way down my spine to where my almost forgotten tail would have been just . . . minutes? . . .

Days? Time had fogged as badly as my vision. It sped up and slowed down and my recollection of the events that took place after that beating is clouded by a rage-filled remembrance of it. I can barely recount it without reaping some poor undeserving Man-monkey's soul as I do.

The scream scared me more than a little. I had no idea what earthly creatures Lilith had created, or was forced to create, since I'd been gone. I now feared that her new "protector" had assumed the role of tyrannical master. There was something that my Great Mother had said to me. And I tried to recall it, but the pain clouded my memory of exactly what it was. *Woman has to—*

A soft moaning voice cut through the silence. Were it not for the fact that it was as familiar to me by then as the black of the night and Adam's beatings, I would have prepared myself for some unknown animal to devour me. As it was, I knew exactly who had come for her evening meal.

"Oh, as I am God in the new Heaven," my Great Mother cawed down at me, "what has become of you, my beautiful Steg?" the voice said. Then Life's light shined and I recoiled from its blistering heat. "Just look at what her imp has inflicted. Oh, your *face! Maddening* Man-monkeys she has created, simply *maddening*. Forgive me, fair fallen angel, you must. . . Here, I shall bring back comforting caress of night."

She dimmed herself, and I tried to look back. "Mother?" I said. I felt certain I knew what would come. I was failing and faltering in the task she had entrusted to me. "I have not fulfilled purpose of app—"

"Shh," her voice was smooth and calming with not a hint of annoyance or frustration in it. "All is well, my beautiful Day Star. You fulfill precious purpose even unaware of those who would seek to see you fail."

I was confused. I groaned and winced my way to sitting up.

Life landed, folded her wings back and then knelt down beside me. She touched my face. "Let us have a look at her murderous Man's miserable work." Then she shook her head slowly. "Ah!" she shouted above her. "He is a ravaging creature best sent to a Hell I must now create to house him. My sister shall. . ." She looked back from the heavens and winced upon seeing my face. "Let us cure your wounds first. They look positively *painful*."

I barely resisted and actually welcomed her touch. It might not have been exactly *who* I wanted, but I definitely needed to feel a soft hand and tender touch on my skin. I had endured terrible touches enough for one—was it one day? "I'm sorry, Great Mother," I said. I truly was. "I haven't delivered your fruit to its purpose. I beg forgiveness. I buried it to hide it from him. Yet, when I returned with them to dig it up as you commanded, it had"—I winced a little as she ran her fingers over my wounds—"the apple had gone missing."

Her hand stroked my cheek like a fine feather tickling my face and I could feel my eye . . . healing? She could heal me! *Why had she not done. . .?* The thought flowed as freely as my blood, and I knew she could hear it.

She touched my jaw. "If I had healed you before," she said, "would lesson of treachery sting its message the same? Or would you have merely waited for your Great Mother to deliver you from evil? I've often wondered if my children will be able to learn of heat and hate without the lesson of fire searing their flesh."

She caressed my face even as my bewilderment grew. Yet I knew that she spoke more to hear the sound of her own words fall upon her ears than she did to have them understood and acted upon. "It is of small consequence," she continued, "for I shall forgive you in your trespasses against me, Steg, as we shall both forgive those who plunder in trespass against us—against sister's poor daughter."

I reached out and pulled her hand from my face before my mind had time to weigh the consequences of resisting my God. "What has happened to Lilith?" I asked. I needed that answer more than the pain could distract me from getting it.

Life sighed and relaxed and I loosened my grip. I could feel her hesitating. "I was afraid of it," she said. "Of . . . what she might do. Yet the Word is the Word and once my sister has written her half of it. . . You see, I am but half of eternity and there is no whole without her, so I suppose we must endure her . . . godly whims.

"If life is to survive the Garden, its creator must be cooperated with. I told you of this not two nights ago. Woman shall serve Man— deliver and endure his every nasty nefarious need. We have Eden's Word to thank for this. Even now her Man brings ruin to fair Lilith's. . . I shudder to think of it. With raping intent her imp violates my own sister's maiden. And to what purpose? . . . Poisonous seed that will come of it? I don't understand it. There are other, gentler ways to deliver life than this. I fear for the eternity to come under her rule, Steg. I truly do."

Do not mistake me, five eternities into Life's treachery, a sane mind would easily see through such devilish deceptions. Yet I had not a single earthly eternity nor edification from having lived in it to guide me.

I had but a three-day-old lust and love and a livid mind clouded by its loss. I was filled with horrible thoughts of a heinous hound hurting that love—no room for a critical thought or a logical action. It was angry thoughts that would guide my hand. I prayed to the surety of the sun rising that it would be enough.

I had been beaten and bruised to a timid mouse. I had no mind for matters of mayhem and murder, it seemed. Those were skills that only Adam was well-versed in applying. It may even surprise you to know that I was more than a little frightened at the prospect of using my face to try and break his fists again.

Centuries later, it occurred to me that my God had not created me for fighting, so much as for fornicating with the frequency of a feral cat.

"Where are they?" I asked my Great Mother, fully realizing that she had forgone her customary "coital toll." Not a night had passed without payment in flesh in order to cross the bridge of yet another of her warmth-filled evenings. And I wondered if she had silently extracted my poison on the two nights I had spent battered and oblivious in the black. "Please, I have to—"

She ran a finger toward my waist—the night's toll would be paid. So for the time that it took the last breaths of the night to expend themselves, my question of whether injury or incapacitation would temporarily stay my love's "tax" was answered with our own "expenditure."

The sun peaked its head up over the horizon and shined through the dense jungle that the Garden had grown to be. It would try in vain to shine one last truth on the deceit that had placed wicked intent in my head and hearts.

But even as the darkness in the Garden gave way to Life's blistering light, the black nothingness she had started, crept its way across my chest, darkening my hearts in preparation for the murder I planned to mete out.

I limped only slightly as I walked, though it was not from Adam's beating. And I could see perfectly fine, thanks to Life's healing touch. Well enough to crush a skull with a rock, I assumed.

That was the method that kept slithering in and out of my thoughts. *Split his Man-monkey head open like a melon and watch his brains spill around his raping body!*

That was what my Great Mother had said Adam was doing to Lilith. I had no idea how I would accomplish it. But my fear of the pain and punishment Adam had already wrought upon my own head was slowly giving way to something else.

The pads of my feet felt the dirt for the first time, and all of my senses drank in the glow of growing life in the Garden. As a parasite pulls precious power from its host, my strength and understanding of mayhem was growing.

My mind became as clouded as my hearts, and by the time my Great Mother, Life, had left me, I was sure that there was more than one "god" of the Garden that needed murdering. "Eden," I said under my breath. If Adam had harmed one hair on the head he was plucked from, I would visit the sins of the son on his true mother . . . right after I cracked open her grandson's skull!

— XI —

I WALKED CLOSER and closer to where my Mother had told me Lilith and Adam were hidden. Or Adam had imprisoned her, was the scenario that ran itself through my thoughts. And all manner of vile violations he could commit worked their way into my imagination. I picked up my pace.

Poor Lilith—a daughter set to the purpose of her demanding god only to be abused and assaulted by the very one she was charged with creating.

It was the fifth day, my Great Mother had informed me, and by that I understood that Lilith should have been deep into creating the creatures of the seas and the oceans. She was to give them the ability to reproduce and run rampant through the waters of the Earth. But the Garden was silent, the only sound I could hear was the inevitable steps that I took toward destruction.

I had little inkling that it would lead to my own.

As I walked, I became aware of . . . creatures . . . watching me. Silent gazes fell upon my back as I passed under trees and vines, and I roughed my way beyond the bushes that had cut my legs not days before. Oblivious to the fresh blood now flowing from my body, I stopped and turned to look at the animals.

Once merely curious, the creatures now cowered and crouched behind scrub brush and trees as I cast my eyes upon them. And I felt a low growl escape my stomach. I had no knowledge of its meaning or intent, but the creatures sensed something . . . something they didn't like.

They quickly fled, scurrying to hiding places and havens unknown, now unseen by me or the light of my Mother's day. And the Garden grew silent again and I was alone. More than that, though, as loneliness was the feeling I now recognized as my sole friend in Eden's great Garden.

Yet, why were the creatures afraid of *me*? I was not a murderous monkey sent to rape and ravage their Mother in nature. I was not a ruinous rat sent to kill them and take them for food. It was more maddening than Life's words had made me feel.

I was but a sage—knowledge-bearing serpent sent to save the Garden from falling to sin and sedition. If they should flee anyone, it should be Adam, not me.

I grew disgusted at their slight of my efforts to spare them. "Flee then, miserable creatures!" I shouted. "Lest you share fate and ferocity with your Man-monkey master! Crawl down into the depths of the Earth if you must, but know this: Abandon me now, and I shall not assist you in your own time of peril. If the fierce fire of this Man-monkey's greed should threaten to engulf *your* house, I shall simply provide more plentiful fuel!"

Nothing stirred . . . and I didn't care.

— XII —

"THEY DON'T FLEE you, Day Star," the voice was one I had only heard once. And Eden buzzed her wings and hovered in the trees above me—out of reach of a fist that I had clenched upon seeing her. "They only feel your hearts and fear for your own loss of them."

I stared hating eyes up at her.

She stared only love back at me. "What heavy intent do serpent's feet pound down on the goodness of the forest floor? What weighs so on your yet to be born soul that you should harbor such hatred this day?"

They were questions I was certain she knew full well the answers to. And if I could lure her down to me, I would reply to them with my own certainty that the only answer to anything she asked would be violence. "How does great God, Eden, send her seed to such a miserable task?" I asked. "You and I grow to serpent the same just as I finally understand my true purpose. Deceitful, distrusting disasters of destruction we are, my *other* Lord! Would you not agree? For if my hearts harbor yet unleashed hatred, then yours have simply beaten me to expelling the vile poison that fills them."

Eden floated, neither losing nor gaining altitude above me.

I looked around me casually, trying not to alarm her as I searched for any way I could climb to her. *Were I still had wings!* I thought.

"You misplace your hatred, fair Steg," she said. "I am not vile villainous creature your Mother whispers me to be."

I had no more mind for plotting, only murder. "May Eden be damned as a liar!" I shouted up at her. "And her precious Garden with her! For if one strand of hair on favored friend's beautiful head be harmed . . . you shall see your wings *torn* from your back!" I breathed harder at the end of it and a real growl—almost a roar—escaped my mouth this time.

Eden remained remarkably calm at my taunts. I felt sure that a direct challenge would bring her within my grasp, but she hovered only slightly lower. "I've written," she said, " 'You shall not take vengeance nor bear a grudge against the sons of your own people.' So, though he be lost and alone, full of hatred and hurt, I shall love my sister's snake as I do my own daughter: I am the Lord, Eden. I would never bring harm upon my own flesh in the Garden. You must sense this even through your Mother's lies."

"Blasphemy escapes your mangy mouth!" I said. "You are not *God* to me. You are but a miserable witch who brings wickedness upon her own daughter." I raged up at her, no idea where the feelings of hatred came from. "If you would hover but lower, green garden *god*, I should cure you of this affliction as I shall cure daughter's spawn of his raping rat ways!"

Eden shook her head. "She has a way in this business," she said. "Of this I am only now becoming keenly aware." Her green glow shined down on me. "She has lied to you, Steg, her Son of the Morning. You are but a child's companion—needed and nethered on top of until she becomes numb to you. Soon, she shall rip out your loving heart and cast it into a pit of pain—throw you aside for another—as sure as you would separate me from head were I to land next to you right now. Of this . . . I can speak only the truth. For you and I, Steg, we are the only ones who may yet save the eternities from her vain and vicious rule. Is this not plain to you? I beg you to see it."

I could see that she had lost the slightest altitude as she spoke. But a little more, and I would plug her mouth with my fist and rip her wings from her back with my teeth if had to. "It is curious to me, witch," I said, "that my Great Mother never speaks of her own sister in this way. Why do you suppose she does not take Lilith's Lord's name to such vanity? Were it so, I would surely call her to task for it." It was a lie, but they were becoming easier for me to tell. And I was becoming as addicted to them as the results they produced.

Eden hovered the slightest distance lower.

As if she sensed my intent, she buzzed back higher and glowed a green to rival any shade of it in the Garden. It almost felt like . . . annoyance or even anger.

She spoke to herself, not to me, "Should I build my great dungeon to damn a hundred of her snakes"—she looked up into the sky at the sun—"she would surely create a thousand of you out of spite." Then she looked back at me. "But what is a thousand to an empty cup with a hole as its bottom? She would never fill up. At ten billion condemned souls I could not hope for her to end it." She stared at me as if she were deciding whether I would be the first soul in the dungeon she muttered of.

I thought it might be my opportunity. "Then flutter your fresh wings to my face and damn me to your dungeon if you must," I said. "I grow weary of standing between such sinful sisters, playing at God." It was a blasphemy against them both and I prayed to the green in the Garden for the safe return of Lilith to my side . . . that my Great Mother had not heard it. I looked past Eden, wondering if my own

God was watching us.

Eden smiled a half frown down at me. I would learn later in life, that the look was not empathy so much as pity for one who is lost to hope and help. "Fear not, Steg," she said, "your Great Mother is . . . devilishly distracted. Though it will take eternities for you to believe me, I ask that you only hear my words. Your Great Mother . . . is not to be trusted. Sadly, it will take time for you to realize this as truth."

I had no idea what she meant, but I didn't like the tone of it. And I had a task to complete. "As you are distracting me from saving Eden's own daughter from her gluttonous Garden. Should you assist me in this, witch, I might consider leaving Lilith's Mother with her head."

She looked down at me curiously and then her face turned to annoyance, scrunching to a form I had not seen on it before. Speaking to her—gazing on her form and face—had been easy since the first time my eyes met hers in the blackness with my Mother.

Eden was a beautiful waif, and bore shades and shape of her daughter that brought forth shadows of the feelings I had for Lilith. But this look on her face was nothing less than disgust . . . directed at me.

"Your gaze turns to a sour green apple," I said to her. "A stark contrast to the sweet cider that spills from my Great Mother's own red ones." It was a truth she could see . . . for I had tasted them both.

Eden's eyes grew wide. "You didn't!" she shouted down. "You cannot! For a Man it is merely—but for serpent to suck the nectar of knowledge? And Life's tree of. . .?" And then her face turned to a knowing of its own.

As it happened, on the very night that I buried Adam's precious fruit, I came upon a gorgeous glen where both glowing green and

ruby red fruits hung so low and appeared so luscious that the temptation to touch them simply could not be resisted. I plucked one of
each, believing that no one, especially Gods distracted in their
heavens, would miss them.

And as it *also* happened, I was correct in this assumption as well.
Eden and Life should've noticed, but . . . how much there is to attend
to as a god!

I would find out later how a god's children and mischief met each
other between the cracks of their parents' distracted attentions. For
while my future sisters worried about each other, I sank a serpent's
fangs deep into their bellies and devoured their devilish desserts down
to nothing but seed and stem.

Shortly afterward, I fell to my knees and vomited the entirety of it,
but their poison was delivered just the same as if I hadn't.

With the green one came the knowledge of good and evil—the
envious goodness of Eden's own understanding and love of her Garden. But from the tree of Life—my God's own precious plant—I was
endowed with eternal life. And *that* meant that I would never die.

To put a more colloquial plain text upon it, I had become a god.
While not equal in power or presence to my now two sisters, never-
theless, neither of them could ever truly be free of me.

It was a truth that Eden knew full well the consequences for its
existence. Her face said as much. "Steg!" she shouted down at me. "It
was forbidden! Did she not tell you of this?" She shook her head. "You
know not what you have done."

"On the contrary, *sister*," I scoffed up at her, grinning as my giddi-
ness only grew, "knowledge is *exactly* what I *do* understand." I tilted
my head to the side and let her feel my resolve. "And now you under-

stand that with that other fruit, and if my earlier warning has gone unheeded, you will have your own 'god' to deal with."

Eden closed her eyes. "Oh, sinful serpent," she said, "you have wrought calamity upon all of Womankind—her Man will run rampant with murder now. She has you in her web, and as the spider approaches to devour us all . . . you revel in a dream of self-deception. You cannot be a god, you are not God! For no one is as long as they once lived.

"This precious palace—the Garden I've built for you all—will run red with coward's blood!" Her wings faltered and sputtered. And as she lost some of her glow, descending slightly as she did. "The faithless, the detestable," she spoke through the tears forming in her eyes, "the murderers, the sexually immoral. . . Sorcerers and idolaters and all the *liars* that they shall bear as children together. . . For your own portion of it, you shall meet them in a lake that burns with fire and sulfur. And constant misery shall be the only death that they will ever know. You, Steg, have condemned humanity to Life . . . and I am now powerless to stop her."

"Lies!" That is what I believed them to be at the time. For once I grew accustomed to hearing them, my mind would not allow me to separate lurid lie from terrible truth. I smiled up at Eden, knowing that I had brought the hopeless feelings in my own hearts to her doorstep and then left them as gifts for her own.

Shortly, Eden's Man-monkey, Adam, would suffer similar fate. "Fear not, sister," I said, "the murdering monkey you have let loose in this heinous hellhole"—I looked in the direction I knew Lilith was being held captive—"will soon be separated from his head. Then he may visit this burning lake that you speak of." I turned and started to walk away.

"No," I barely heard her voice behind me. I stopped and turned around, but my ears only recognized the last words Eden spoke to herself, ". . .already killed her, forgotten Protector." Then she looked at me. "Oh all my godly power. . . You have failed her in this, Eden. Failed miserably."

Yet I remained confident in my new revelation. For I had let Adam beat and pound me, believing that there was some divine purpose to my persecution. But I knew now that his was an insidious affliction, cured only by separation of his body from his head. "Fret no more," I said to Eden, "I shall protect your fair daughter far more effectively than the raping monster you wrought upon her."

She shook her head slowly at me. "How could I have been so. . .?" I could see green glowing tears running down her fairy-white face and it struck me as more than simply her, having to share godliness, would bring.

I tilted my head and frowned at her. "Shed not tear for young Adam, fair sister," I said, "I shall crop his sinful serpent as well. Then I may allow you to rejoice with Lilith again . . . if it please me."

Her wings sputtered and buzzed back and forth, hesitating her in mid-air. "I shall never see precious daughter as Woman in nature again," she said. "Because of your gluttony"—her eyes locked onto my own, painfully staring at me as if begging my words to be false—"my lovely Lilith is already dead."

I stood in the clearing beneath the trees where Lilith had attacked then straddled me on that first morning. The flora of her once beautiful and hopeful Garden seemed more ashen gray than green now.

The Garden was ours then, if only for one day. And it was a promising place of play that her Great Mother, Eden, had built to house love and lusciousness—creations and creatures to rival my own God's stars in number and brightness.

I tried to remember the feelings that had warmed my body and yet unborn soul. The thoughts and desires that had stiffened my snakes and sent my eyes to Lilith's beautiful pink body and her lightly-hued hair. . . Those feelings were as absent as color was now.

I watched in silent rage, a mind filled with images and thoughts of ruin and rape and now regret, as Lilith's eyes turned from giddy and gorgeous to the final shades of ghastly gray—ghosts. Eden had tried to warn me. Now her own egg. . . The truth was before me—rawly split open from its fragile shell—and her daughter, Lilith, lie blood-spilled and dead.

Lilith's body was roughed and ravaged with scratches and scrapes, and blood no longer flowed from her wounds, having long since expended itself onto the dirt beneath our sap trees. Now, everything about her—everything I knew and had loved—was crimson spent life mixed with dirt. She was nothing left but bloody mud—the essence of what remained of my hearts.

I knelt down beside her and lifted her limp body to my lap. I brushed a little of her hair from her face even as tears overflowed the bottoms of my eyes. They dripped onto her face and I watched the death of my own compassion roll down her cheeks and fall to the ground, mixing with her mud. And the acid that I felt burn into my hearts on that day was nothing compared to the burning fire I would rain down upon Adam . . . and his children, should he live to bear any. The thought of it made me roar above my head as I now know lions to do.

It seemed I had been too slow to anger. A mistake that I vowed never to repeat again. For though I had abounded in forgiveness, even for the sin and rebellion of the Man-monkey, Adam, I had mistakenly left the guilty unpunished. Another of my unrepeatable sins. One that had cost my love, Lilith, her precious life.

Yes, Adam would die, as certainly as I now had all the time of every eternity to make sure of it. And I would punish his children for the sin of their pathetic parent to the third and fourth . . . and the *fifth* generation's eternities to repay him. There would be no Man birthed or created that I would spare this wrath.

And they would know no God but me. As soon as I dealt with my two new sisters.

LOSS

— XIII —

I SAT UNDER our trees, silently brooding as the rest of the Garden went back about its business, copulating and creating life. Lilith's limp body still in my lap. I had time to get to Adam. Where could he run? Yet he *was* gone.

I think even he realized the finality of what he had done. There would be nowhere for him to. . . Now, three gods looked to spike an olive branch of "peace" through his head.

As I would find many times throughout my existence, often the only thing that your God will leave you to fight for, will be a bitter-sweet ashen thirst for revenge, gritting its way around and between your teeth and gums. A sooty but seductive substitute for a lifetime of guilt over sin. Everything would be made this way. Save bowing and scraping your knees bloody at their feet, that is.

For that, the only punishment would be an unknown Purgatory at the end of Life's miserable life. *My Great Mother.* . . I pondered the thought. Had she deceived me as her sister, Eden, had said? Was Life devil and not my all-loving deity? I tried to replay all of her words in my head.

Hidden meanings and maniacal intentions sifted in and out of my mind. It could not be. Eden on the other hand. . . My fair Lilith's Mother had spoken truth, as I was beginning to understand its feel in my ears. She had not attacked me, had not molested me in any way, figurative nor literal, as my Great Mother was so prone to do.

To ferret out and figure the truth of it, as the sun slowly set over the Garden, I awaited my "love's" arrival, lying on my back.

Sowing seeds, I thought, staring up into my Mother's stars. Both of my new sisters were obsessed with it. The seeds of luscious green life in the Garden, the seeds of a Man-monkey pumped and penetrated into the Woman I loved, the seeds of knowledge and eternal life that I had stolen from them both. . . *I shall show you seed to sow*, I thought.

For if sowing seeds was how the godly game of gluttony was played, then I would learn it, live it, and eventually come to love the reaping of all the seeds that any of us would ever sow. But first, before any sowing or revenge-filled reaping could ever take place, a sinful seed needed to be planted inside fertile soil—deep inside a warm and wet womb. A place where it could crack open and grow to a precious parasite, both needing and eating its host alive.

If the godly universe wanted babies to birth, I would burn and boil and bake babies into both of my sisters until the Garden drowned beneath gobbling gums.

I looked up into the branches above me at the failing light of the . . . *fifth* day, was it? I had no idea what would happen on the seventh. Lilith did—she had tried to tell me as much. She was dead.

I could see the flickering bright light of one of the Gods who might be at least partially responsible for that fact. The flicker grew brighter, descending from the Heavens—a sky and brightness that Life most surely had created by then. I wondered what it must be like up there, and then I smiled, wondering what it would look like . . . once I burned it down to the Garden's ground.

* * *

Life landed next to me only a few feet from Lilith's body. My "love" looked at my true one and then over at me. Her brightness was easier to endure now. She seemed less than surprised to see Lilith lying dead.

I had rolled Lilith's body on its side—her face and once beautiful eyes turned away from me—not being able to completely part with what was left of her, but not wanting to see her eyes during my Mother's coital visitation either.

I would do what had to be done. I knew Lilith would understand. I hoped she would understand.

It was too long before Life spoke to me. I imagined that she mulled tactics and tact in her mind, unsure of which direction a sound strategy should take her. Yet the one inevitable thing she had come for, was now something that my own strategy required as much as her lusting loins did.

"And how fares my Great Mother on this eve of her niece's destruction?" I asked. It was spiteful to be sure, but I was coming to realize that tyrants loved any interest in their own welfare more than prudence would allow them to subdue.

"I am"—she hesitated only briefly, looking down at Lilith's body and then back at me—"less than fine at the end of this terrible and so tragic fifth day of my sun in the Garden." She shook her head slowly, I imagined she was merely playing her part. "As my light gives way to the comforting, and I *so* hope consoling, warmth of my sister's. . . Steg, I stand stunned at her failure. I simply have no words." She looked back at Lilith's body. I could hardly stand to have her near it. "And I am saddened by the events that I see have transpired since I last met with you."

"Met" with me. . . The thought burned rage into me. She would

pull her ounce of poison from me, voyeuristic corpse to view as she did or not.

I forced a smile up at her. I wanted that poison delivered as much as she did. "Saddened?" I asked. "Are you, mother?" I would put on a good show before I "let" her have me. "Sister's maiden lies murdered and the perpetrator runs raping wild in her garden even as we speak!

"Who knows what beast he has found to mount and then murder this night. I've failed you, mother!" It would be better if she believed I was more regretful of that. "As I've failed Lilith." I looked at her body, but then had to look away lest my hearts trip the trigger on my trap too soon.

"I had no idea that Adam would—" she stopped herself and knelt next to Lilith's body.

I sat up quickly, lurching and almost losing my composure as she touched Lilith's hair. I wanted to rip into her—rape her for the rape that she had so obviously allowed to happen to Lilith. There was nothing left in my hearts but darkness—black coal to mine and use to stoke the fire of my hatred to a flaming red inferno. But I gathered myself.

Revenge would be a long and twisting road, and I had more eternities to drive Life down it than she realized. "Can you. . .?" I knew she could. The apple from the tree of knowledge told me as much.

"Not without *great* cost," she said. She would lead with the lies and see where my response took them. I knew her well enough by then to see it.

"To whom?" I asked. "For as Adam is her murderer so shall he repent and repay."

She pulled her hand from Lilith's hair and I relaxed. Then she fluttered her wings and floated inches off the ground, landing next to me. "Oh, Steg," she said, folding her wings behind her as was her way before she mounted me, "you cannot control the Heavens or how the eternities play themselves out. I warned you this would happen. I warned you of her. My sister's jealousy reaches past her and down into her precious offspring as well. I fear she is afflicted with it . . . terminally. Lilith's Man-monkey has not slain her, he is merely knife wielded by holy hand of hatred and vanity."

I could feel her touching me and my snakes stiffened. I would endure it one final time to the purpose of delivering the venomous poison that would unleash destruction and misery on my God's children forever.

It was over none too quickly for the bitter taste of disgust that grew in my mouth. And Life pulled herself off of me and spread her wings, shaking herself loose of our lust. She turned from me and looked at Lilith's body. "In time," she said softly, "you will come to listen to my commands and take heed of my warnings as they are given. Were it so this day, fair niece might still draw breath. As it is, I shall return fallen angel to Heaven . . . and we shall speak no more of her for at least an eternity."

She was taking her? "Wait!"

Life spun at me and screeched so loudly that I grabbed my ears. Then her black eyes glowed as a wild animal looks at another that is threatening to takes its meal. "We shall *not* discuss it!" she shouted. "It is the only way your precious Lilith will continue. As angel to do bidding of her God in Heaven.

"Tomorrow, I shall replace sister's failure with a Woman of my own, and she will woo and offer her womb to Adam, so that this putrid pit of pestilence will birth *my* children and know *me* as their only God!"

The eternal trouble with the truth is, that as Life always does, it finds a way to shine itself through the darkest of deceptions, even the ones we perpetrate on ourselves.

As the next day was the sixth, I wanted to know how. . . "When and how shall I help?" I asked. My seditious seed had been delivered. I knew that as certainty. I felt it pass between us. Now, I needed to distract my Great Mother from detecting it as it worked its poison into her womb.

How long it would take for that poison to infect her and eat her hearts from the inside. . .? Infect hers as she had infected and devoured mine? I didn't care. I had nothing but the everlasting time of the eternities on my side to find out.

Life picked up Lilith's lifeless corpse and turned to face me. "By the next eve in sister's Garden," Life said to me, "you shall know of my daughter, Steg, and you shall guide her to Adam for his seed to be planted inside her womb. And as I've told you before, she shall be his wife. Then as Adam submits to me as his only God, so also shall Eve submit in everything to her husband. And this shall be the fate of Woman and the new beginning for my sister's faltering and festering Garden."

In less time than it took for me to understand the magnitude of my God's deception of me, she flapped her wings wildly and streaked up into the stars. Gone . . . along with the last ounce of doubt I harbored that I would kill Adam in the morning.

— XIV —

HIGH ATOP THE Great Mountain of the Eternities, inside the Throne Chamber of the Protectors—Eden's own residence in her sister's newly created Heaven—Life stood in front of her sister. She held Lilith's lifeless body in front of her as Eden wept openly.

Eden reached out and gently took her daughter's body from Life. Then she somberly climbed the granite steps to her perch.

The huge rock-carved chair wore a chiseled-in-stone shield and sword—the Sword of Power. It formed the reclining back of the Throne of Judgment.

The Throne of Judgment. . . That was its name and that was the task and duty of the one who occupied it. A duty that, all too often and throughout the eternities to come, would require the meting out of punishment for the crime of murder.

"I am sorry, sister," Life said. "I have no words for it, only sorrow in my hearts. I fear I've completely misjudged my serpent's disposition in fair sister's—he has simply. . . I realize that you warned me of th—"

"Silence!" Eden screeched. It was a rare loss of composure that took Life completely by surprise, as it did every newly minted or gilded gold angel in the room. For it seemed that the sisters had both been busy creating and crowning followers to protect their Protectors.

Two freshly minted and glowing-green Garden Guardian Angels flanked Eden on either side of her throne, and two newly gilded *Golden* Guardians stood on either side of Life. The sharp shining feathers on all four of them spoke of war more than warmth now. And to a last angelic one of them, they all slammed their wings behind them and pushed out steel feathers and long talons at Eden's screams.

"I shall hear no more of this!" Eden said. "For precious daughter has been slain and"—she looked deeply into Life's black eyes—"and as her body grows cold in my arms, I shall *not* speak of blame. For it is upon us, sister. As surely as your sun will set at the end of the day"— she closed her eyes as she sat on the throne—"blame is surely upon us all."

The bright orange sun of Life's warmark, in *her* soon-to-be Heaven if she had her way, burned brightly from the shields on the backs of her followers. And the deep green heart-shaped shamrocks of Eden's Garden warriors glowed mint and unlucky misery back for anyone who would dare threaten their Great Mother of nature.

Life eyed the two Green Guardians. They would be easy prey for her snakes. Though in her present mind of rage and ruin, her sister would not. Regardless, it was not yet the time, and she had a plan for ridding herself of the only one perching between her and the throne she knew she deserved. "I understand how you feel considering your hope for the great—"

"You know *nothing* of it!" Eden shouted. "You and your snakes!" She would play the part she needed to, as she was not the only one in the room who knew how Lilith had truly met her ending—Eden had been with her sister's snake as it happened. She looked next to Life at her latest play toy. "You and your filthy fornicating serpents," she said. "I should make them slither on their bellies through the guts of my Garden. Through all the eternities they will suffer for this crime!" She stared down at her daughter's lifeless mortal being and rocked back and forth on her throne. Eden's tears streaked and poured down on Lilith's face. When she looked back up at Life, there was more than hatred in her eyes. "As surely as anyone who had a hand in this shall *burn* on a cross . . . as spectacle and warning for sin!"

Life turned to one of her Golden Guardians—her newest one—a serpently sinner himself. He *was* delectable, and it would be a loss, yet one that she could easily replace. She looked at his long blonde locks and then into his deep gray eyes. He was more boy than the manhood she had extracted from him upon the first eve of his birth. "Forgive me, fair Norl," she said, moving in closely to his breast. "You have barely tasted all that this short time with your God has to offer. Yet sadly"—she pushed out every sharp feather on her body, her long talons shot from her fingers, and then she shoved both of her hands into Norl's chest and ripped out his hearts before he knew or noticed what she had done—"your time with me has ended."

And Norl's barely days-old beating hearts dripped black and red blood from Life's hands even as his body slammed to the floor and sprayed pointless lost life across Eden's throne room.

Both of Eden's guardians hardened all of their armored feathers. They prepared to spin and send as many ballistic feathered-arrows at their God's sister as it would take to stop her if she attacked. And Life's remaining Golden Guardian did the same—though who he was more afraid of facing in a fight for his life was no longer clear to him.

Life looked at her remaining guardian and scoffed. She leaned in toward him and whispered in his ear, "Fear not, pretty serpent," she said, "you have precious venom yet left in your vile." She ran her hand to his waist. "An affliction we shall remedy on this very last eve of creation."

Eden stood up. Her guardians raced down the first few steps in front of her throne to protect her. "For all innocence that's holy, sister!" she shouted. "One eternity. . . Someday one of them will do more than fill thy womb with ecstasy. You simply cannot keep *killing* them! Sinful snakes though they may be or not. This is the madness I hoped to—"

"Is this not the Word you have written in our book?" Life asked. She gazed calmly and curiously back at her sister. "Do we not offer eye for eye, tooth for tooth"—she pointed at Lilith's dead body—"and precious tail of serpent for treason against fallen sister's own servant? Pray tell me now and I shall offer up alternate penance for the slight of my soon to be dealt with Steg in your garden." She looked at her remaining guardian angel and frowned at him. "Sadly"—she turned back to her sister—"my guardians have yet to find what rock he has hidden himself under. Had they, I would have offered his own spiked head as payment for your waif."

Eden knew she had to find Steg before her sister did. For he was the only other soul who knew as she did—it had been Life who took Lilith's from her. She also knew that any ounce of understanding she showed would touch off the war that was, to date, only brewing in her seditious sister's mind. She was not ready for it, not yet. She tilted her head up and looked at the ceiling. "Find him!" she screeched out in pain. It was the only command she could give without raising suspicion.

— XV —

THEY CAME IN the middle of the sixth day. Two of them, golden and shining as brightly as my God's sun—one dark-haired and the other as fair as Eden's fairies.

I knew she had to do something, for to return to Heaven with a dead daughter as a gift from her sister's Garden could only be met with wrathful rage. And these warriors were birthed and bred for one thing. Or so I believed from the look of them. They were simply assassins, sent by my own Mother to kill me. Angels to be certain—wings and talons as sharp as my own had been. Yet curiously absent tails at the base of their backs.

I remembered my own tail and for the first time I lamented its loss. But I had lost far more precious things in the week since my birth and rebirth into Eden's Garden. I had yet to find the Man-monkey that had taken those things from me. Now, in addition to his seeming skill at hiding from me, Adam had two angel guardians between him and his severed head.

Yet by day six, I knew the depths of the Garden far better than the two flying monkeys my mother had sent. After I planted my poison and my Great Mother left me, I had scoured the depths of Eden's jungle for the rest of the night and most of the next morning. I searched in vain for the murdering hand that killed Lilith.

I had just stopped to rest in the shadow of a huge boulder when I heard them, wings rushing and whistling as they landed in the tall grass not a stone's throw away from my hiding place.

They were young. Younger than I was or thought myself to be. Their bewilderment upon arriving in what to them was a foreign land, was probably as confusing as their understanding of the black before their birth. I understood more than they did about that, I was certain. And I knew something else. Even if they succeeded in murdering me, I would not die.

Their arrival confirmed one thing—my Great Mother God would sacrifice me if it suited her purposes. And . . . she had had some hand in Lilith's death. I gritted my teeth and pursed my lips to keep the growl from escaping.

"Tell me again," the dark-haired one said to the other, "*what* became of young Norl?"

The second one—the fairer of the two—looked nervously around him as if his answer would bring forth wrath and lightning. He may not have known it, but he was not far from truth in his assessment of the peril that lay in wait too close to him for his own good. "She ripped out his hearts," the second one said. "In front of sister and all angels' eyes."

"I don't believe this for one moment," the darker assassin said. "Why would she do such a thing? Norl has never offered reason for —"

"Were you there?" the fair one asked. "Did angel's own eyes drink in the lust and livid larceny as she stole his life from him? Mine own eyes witnessed it! She is *mad*, I tell you. We will all burn because of it."

The dark one looked around. I could smell the guilt wafting through the air. "Thankfully," he said, "I was not. And you would do well to hold tongue inside of mouth lest, from the sounds of your tale, our Great Mother cut it out."

"Then take my mind from thoughts of unforgettable past," said the lighter angel, "and assist me in finding this present murderer, or as sure as Norl is dead, we shall suffer his same fate."

I watched motionless as the lighter one looked around, only one of his hearts on his task. No doubt the other worried for its safety, trying to make sure that it was not ripped from under his breast, pulled out by my Great Mother's now apparently insatiable appetite for blood. Whomever and wherever poor Norl might be, this assassin cared not to join him. "Eye for an eye," he muttered, looking around the tall grass.

"Or 'head on a pike' she said," replied the dark-haired one.

My head . . . on a pike? Such was my introduction to the true love of my God. A spiked head for her own hand, inciting murder against her sister.

That was my new understanding of the Garden. How life would flourish in less than one day's time, I hadn't the slightest idea. There seemed to be only death or the intent of it everywhere I looked.

"Steg," the whispering voice was unmistakable, and every muscle in my body tensed and my jaw clenched tightly. "Who are they?" the bush just to the side of my rock, barely into the sunshine next to it, spoke. It was Adam, and it took everything I had not to rush at him.

I peered into his hiding place and my eyes squinted and then widened slightly. Without a doubt in my mind, he had been mere feet away, preparing to bash in my head as I had planned to separate him from his.

I could just make out his murdering Man-monkey eyes beneath the hanging branches of the bush. I spoke at him as softly as my anger and rage, but pressing need not to get caught, would allow, "I should pop out your eyes and rip them from your sockets, monkey," I tried not to hiss at him, "for precious blood spilled in this Garden."

"What are you blathering about, snake?" he replied, growing more nervous and raising his voice louder than I thought safe. "The only blood I have let is yours."

"Then why do you hide, imp?" I tried to whisper back.

He pointed at the two angels, now searching in vain, haphazardly meandering about as the day's shadows grew long. "I knew *they* would come."

"Yes, they would come," I said only just softly enough, moving closer to his hide as I did. Perhaps I could silently grip his throat and choke the life from his eyes without too much noise. Turn him a ghostly gray as he had done to Lilith. "*They* have come to deliver murdering monkey"—I looked back toward the grass field then back at Adam—"to my Great Mother—see you beheaded for killing fair daughter."

"What madness are you afflicted with?" he whispered back. "You are drunk on your own poison. Were they to do that, I should be delivered to the very one who slay her."

Now his lies were starting to infect into my mind, and I paused. But something under his words. . . There was not lying voice in them, and I was becoming better at sorting truth from tall tale. "My own. . .?"

I didn't want the answer for the task it would bring, but I knew it as certain as the next words Adam spoke. "Yes, all-knowing serpent," his voice tried to remain calm. "I witnessed your Great Mother's talons pierce her to death myself"—he looked around nervously, through the dense branches of his hiding bush—"just before she left to copulate with her favorite snake. Tell me, was my wife's warm womb even cold as you mated with that monster?"

I could stand it no longer. I burst from the shadow of my boulder and dove into the bush and tackled into Adam. And I felt roar after roar escape my lips, uncontrollable growls that raged to sink fangs and pump poison into my Lilith's ravaging Man. And Adam tried to fight back, but I had a renewed hatred and hot fiery resolve to end him.

My fists and teeth and feet punched and bit and kicked into him as he had assaulted and beaten me before. And I violated him with harsh hands on his snake, as I was sure that he had violated my fair Lilith with it.

I cared not for the two angel assassins who would surely capture us both now. For if I knew anything as I beat at Adam's flesh, I knew that he had told the truth . . . and that now we were as good as heads on those angels' pikes.

— XVI —

ADAM AND I both knelt, though being forced to your knees in front of. . . There had to be thousands of squawking and cawing, and screeching and screaming angels perched along the sides of the huge arena. And we were the center of their attention. Soon, very soon, I felt as if we would both meet back with Lilith in the black. At least that is what I knew it must have felt like to Adam. I would suffer a different, far less certain, fate.

Adam's eye was blackened and as swollen shut as mine had been, and he looked simply defeated, squatting naked next to me. His snake certainly showed no signs of fight. Not that my own were any more ready for battle than his. He coughed blood in front of him, and a golden angel kicked him and he fell sideways, moaning in pain.

I smiled. It was good for Adam to feel helpless for a change. But he had been correct. As soon as the two angel assassins in Eden's Garden had heard the commotion we made as I beat him, they pounced on us, beat us both to a senseless, sinful pile of pulp and poisonous intent, and then flew us back to a gone-insane new Heaven.

The pair of angel assassins debated lopping off our heads with their wings, but neither of them had the stomach or staunch resolve to risk cheating our Great Mother. If Life had been so inclined to want to chop my head off personally, they wouldn't be the ones to deprive her of it.

I spit some of my own blood in front of me and took a golden angel's foot to my guts for it.

And the crowd of—my Great Mother God had been busy. Thousands of angels screeched from everywhere, it seemed to me. I pushed myself back to my knees and looked up above the center of the huge hall and field. We looked to be spectacle for the sport of a crowd. That would not end well for whomever my Mother pitted me against.

I could see her brightness, hovering above the center of the . . . arena. There were two golden angels beneath her on the floor of the field. I wondered if Eden had told her the truth I had divulged not days before. If she had, my Mother would surely be working on something to take my eternal life. If the fruit from the tree of knowledge had told me anything, it was that the pomp of power didn't like to share lavish limelight.

And that fact made me pause. I gazed at the entire circumference of the arena. Were it not for the severed heads of at least ten green fairies and waif angels—Eden's own children in Heaven—shoved down upon tall standing pikes, mouths drooped open waiting for flies to light in them and lay maggot-making eggs, there would have been no hint that my great God's sister, Eden, ever existed.

"For the crime and sin of sedition," Life spoke in a booming voice, "and the subversion of the great Garden of Life. . ." She was going to sink her fangs right into the sin of the week.

The crowd quieted to a sound as silent as my first night in the Garden had been. And the one who had visited me and taken my venom and virginity was now going to deflower someone from their life.

She continued, "And for the death of fair daughter, Lilith—Woman, the violation of our common covenants and the wanton war against the Word of your great God, Life. . ." She wasn't even going to attempt concealing her arrogance and deception. Life placed lie and lips that they fell from in front of every feathered faithful follower she had obviously birthed from the black for that very purpose.

It was an army of angels, all loyal and all resembling more zombi-fied zealot in Heaven than clear-thinking creature of the cosmos. And if there was one more thing that the fruit of knowledge had provided me, it was that a follower's feathers would be seared in the flames of their master's whims and whimsy . . . before they ever smelled the smoke or felt the flames as they burned.

To a mindless minion, carrying out murder and mayhem for their masters, their gods were devils by any other name.

A tremendous roar erupted through the grandstands—cawing and crowing and calls for death and destruction reached a pitch that stung into my ears. I jerked my head up to look at all of them.

The closest angels—the ones at the very edges of the huge arena—seemed to be looking past me at something. I bent over and tilted my head down to look between and through my legs, behind me. There was an approaching prisoner.

For if the great God, Eden, was anything now—shackled in iron manacles, being poked and prodded by the wings of six golden gilded guards all around her—she was most surely a prisoner of her younger sister's army. A sister who now showed nothing but the truth of her own seditious intentions, completely confident in mid-coup, green with envious greed and giddy at her elder sister's plummet from power.

I had played part and parcel of mayhem and message in the

Garden, just as I now understood that there were precious few around me who had not.

Adam looked as bewildered by the sight of Eden in chains as I did. He quickly turned away and would not look at her again.

Certainly she had some power to resist? She was the great God of her eternity, Eden of the Garden. *Shouldn't she do something?* The thought only lasted until the next assault of accusations flew from my Great Mother's lips.

"For the death of her own daughter," Life's voice boomed her lying blasphemy for any and all to hear, "and the rape and ruin of the genesis of your God, Life," she shouted, "our Great Mother of Nature, Eden, has been stripped of her godly gifts. And shall now suffer fate of annihilation!"

At that, the crowd of crows in the grandstands went insane. Screeching and screaming and cawing for Eden's head to join her followers' severed ones—spiked on a pike at the edge of the arena.

I looked at Eden, now shoved to her knees between Adam and me. Her shame and helplessness weighed as heavy on her as her sagging shoulders pulled at her limp and wilting wings.

It was obvious that she had been beaten and tortured . . . badly, but from the looks of the blood running down her legs, she had also been —*They wouldn't*, I thought. I knew it was another lie I was telling myself. Because as hard and as long as I stared straight at her, Lilith's great God Mother, Eden of the Garden, only cowered—she would not meet my gaze upon her shame of violation. My great God, Life, had turned to a venomous violating villain.

I looked past Eden at Adam, himself staring straight down at the floor of this great hall of injustice. And a question gnawed at my hearts. It was answered with Life's next indictment.

"Behold," Life said, "here is my once virginal sister and her concubine. I bring them out now from Eden's own Dungeons of Damned souls to show you their shame and guilt."

Concubine? I thought. *I was not any. . .*

Life was enjoying herself, but her accusations could have just as easily been cast in a mirror for her own actions and assaults on me. And yet she continued in her hypocrisy, "For I've violated them both as they have done to each other. I've allowed you to do with them what seemed good to you. And you have shown them the adulterous folly of their wicked ways."

I had no idea what she was speaking of, because I had only ever been venomously violated by her and—*No. . .* The thought astounded me. I looked at Adam—stared at him until he felt my gaze upon his cowering carcass.

When he turned his eyes toward me, the guilt oozed from him as sure as his seed had slithered its way into my fair Lilith's mother.

I looked over at Eden. She still offered neither opposition nor protest to the claims or her chains. She was a disgraced deity, damned to her own dungeons.

But I didn't understand it. If Eden was criminal—and as angered and disgusted as I was at the thought of it, the truth was clear that she *was* guilty. . . But by that measure, my Great Mother was as guilty as the green God next to me. By thrice orders of sin at the very least. Which was to say nothing of the nights I could not remember and my own part in all of it.

I looked at Life and her black eyes met mine. She grinned only slightly at me before turning her face back to stone seriousness. I was her pawn in strategy, and she prepared to sacrifice me again as she already had for her own game and gain. I smiled down at the gem-studded floor in front of me. *My secret will. . .* I hoped it *would* save me, for it had yet to be tested.

I knew that the seed I had delivered was working its way to the fruit it would bear inside my God Mother's womb. But if this were the house it would be born into, I had no doubt that Life would make any offspring she conceived, suffer and die in the darkness of her deceit. She was obviously prepared to do it to anyone who rivaled her.

The three of us were lost. The best part of any of our treacherous souls, lay dead somewhere in Life's web of lies and deceit—God only knew what fate would befall my precious Lilith. For the once indignant Eden was now kneeling in a shadow of her own treachery, carried out even as her daughter toiled and was tortured.

Eden's Garden concubine, Adam, was but a short distance on the other side of her. And I . . . I was in the most precarious position of all the poison flowing that day. Stuck sinfully in the middle between sister and sinning sister—the only truth left—a mirror to the web of lies that my God, Life, was spinning.

And that is another thing about lies, depending on who is telling them. . . The larger the life is that is force-feeding them, the easier they are for simpletons to swallow. The grandstands in the arena appeared to be packed with *those* beings.

An involuntary growl escaped my lips, and I took a foot to the back of my head and fell face forward and split open my lip. The sweet copper taste of salty sin slipped into my mouth and I swirled it around and then swallowed it. I would waste no more of my own blood trying to turn the color of their lies. They flowed as a waterfall of taint, down from Life's lips, spilling into the arena like black oil that would never wash off. It would take more than one eternity to clean my own feathers of them.

— XVII —

DEEP BENEATH THE great Arena of Reckoning. . . There had been a reckoning for certain. And as I stood alone in my cell in Eden's newly created Dungeon of the Damned. . . A place I had no doubt she would never have conceived herself imprisoned. . . But as I pressed my bloodied face tight against the iron bars on the gate of my cell, I had no idea why my death had not come.

I touched the great seal on the lock. The searing sun of Life's mark burned into my fingers. *She shall burn you as she did*—and I wondered if a "god" would or could resurrect from fire. I had no idea at the time what "annihilation" meant.

Because shortly after Life was finished with her list of accusations and verbal assaults on her sister and Adam, she motioned for her guardians to drag them to their feet. Still other angels wheeled in huge carts with trees they had harvested from the Garden.

They had to be from the Garden as Life's Heaven seemed as bleak and barren as her absent soul. I feared my seed may have been planted in an ashen wasteland of wanton lust in Life's womb. It might never grow there.

When the golden angels tipped those carts up, the trees inside them were lashed together with vines into huge crosses. The echoes of Eden's screams as angels pounded spikes into her feet and hands, nailing her to those rough-sawn sap trees, still echoed in my mind. Adam was no less vocal as they drove iron spikes through his murdering hands and feet.

Though, piecing the power struggle together, I had finally figured out—more accurately, I had accepted—that the screeching in the Garden that night. . . Just before my Great Mother had taken her tax in venom from my snakes, she had spiked her talons into Lilith's flesh.

She killed Lilith as surely as Adam had tried to make me understand it. It was of little consequence that I forgave him for it as they nailed him to his cross, for only seconds later the angels lit them both on fire and burned them, sap-tree crosses and all, to a gray pile of ash on the floor of the arena.

Not one angel in the grandstands would have been able to hear the crackle of cooking flesh and feathers above the screams of Eden and her concubine Man-monkey, not a single one of them . . . but me. I shall never forget it.

Fire is the most miserably murderous way to die. And I vowed that one day, I would see Life burn for killing my maiden, Lilith.

What misery and murder gods bring down upon their children, I thought. It all seemed a pointless pomposity to me, and none of it brought me any closer to having Lilith back, or killing the one responsible for her death.

My God and I were the only ones left who knew the truth of it. Soon she would have to change that. Because sinful secrets have but one rule if they be kept that way—no one else should know them.

For the present moment, my God had her secret locked down underneath the Arena of Reckoning in her dead sister's dungeon. But even the darkest dungeons had ears to cast truth, and then sow the seeds of doubt toward one's God.

— XVIII —

THE DARKNESS IN the dungeon was more black than the nothingness I was birthed from, and I shook at the bars on my cell. I would not escape that way.

"Where are we?" the voice spoke in a tone as familiar to me as it was sweet.

"Lilith!" I couldn't stop myself from shouting. I rushed to the edge of my cell and tried to look down the dark tunnel toward her voice. I could see nothing.

I put my arm through the bars and reached and stretched my hand toward her. It . . . it couldn't be! I'd held her lifeless corpse in my own arms!

"I ask again," she spoke. The sound as sweet to me as the apples I had stolen and stripped clean in the Garden.

"We're in my envious and evil God's talons," I said. "Firmly ensnared in a trap of treachery and taint." I squinted my eyes, but could not see to the voice or cell but a few feet to the side of mine. "How are you here? I feared you . . . you were dead."

"Dead?" she said. "I haven't lived but this day. Why would I be dead?" Her voice was as truthful and genuine as it had been, and her bewilderment was real.

"Lilith?" I asked. Perhaps she was hallucinating again. For all I knew I might be in the black of a dream after being burned on a cross.

"What woman shares cell and scent with us?" she said. "Who is

Lilith?"

The rage began building in me again. My great God, Life? Had she resurrected the object of my love only to strip her mind that I ever existed? A treachery more torturous than her death had been.

Would I have to hear her voice as penance and punishment for my own God's sins? Was this to be my fate? Locked in a dungeon, inches away from the sweet nectar of love, not a drop to taste or touch? *Torment!*

"Lilith!" I couldn't contain it. "You're Lilith of the God Eden's Great Garden. And I . . . I. . ." For some reason the word would not come. I was hallucinating it. I prayed to a yet unborn son inside Life, that he be born and burn her! Nail her to a cross as she'd spiked Eden and Adam.

"Are you Adam?" the beautiful voice asked me.

The name burned like acid into my hearts. I thought nothing left of them but they had lit up with hope at hearing Lilith's voice, only to catch fire and sear burning misery into me at her lost memory of who I was. And Adam, I was most *certainly* not. "He's dead." I cared not if the revelation hurt her. I wanted him nothing but gone since he arrived. "He shall violate you no more." I debated informing her of the treachery that he had hidden under her very nose in the Garden's now marred and murderous beginning.

For no matter how future protectors would tell the tale, Eden's great Garden had quickly turned from genesis to genocide. I feared the taint on it would never wear off.

There was no response from the voice. Seconds passed before she spoke. "I was. . ." her voice hesitated as if trying to find truth in what she may have believed to be lies. "Adam and I are to seed Life's

Garden," she said. "My Great Mother, God, informed me of this. I believed you to be Adam. Are you another of my Great Mother's serpent sages? Will you guide and guard me in her Garden?"

Great Mother, I thought. I wondered if this waif—I was coming to the acceptance that Lilith had been replaced. Life had gelded her green sister, grabbed the Garden for herself, and prepared to restart its genesis with this—"The question is," I said to her, neither sensing nor knowing the answer I would get. . . In the hindsight of eternities, I would not want to have known. But curiosity kills all caution. It is an . . . eternal truth. "My own question is, who are you?"

If a spike had been driven into my heart, the next words she spoke could not have pained me more. "I'm the wife-to-be of Adam in my Great Mother, Life's, Garden," she said. "I am Eve."

LIES

— XIX —

EVE. . . IT WAS a damning truth, and by my calculations an imminent one. For if she was to finish the task of seeding Life's thoroughly bastardized thicket of thieves and murderers on the Earth. . . Lilith's mind turned to a zombified Eve or not, there was but one day left for either of them to complete the task.

I hung my head and let the loss burn into me. Cook every last ounce of anything that would ever be good again and leave me an ashen wasteland of wickedness and war.

If my God wanted to play devilish deity. . . If Life wished to see me suffer in her game, she would view what godly immortality could truly do when fueled by hatred and jealousy. I would not bow, nor scrape, nor play the doting feeble-minded moron as her mounting minions had been birthed to. I would become devil . . . in any hell she could conjure.

In any system—be they rulers in Heaven or governments of Man-monkey morons—the "gods" that design that system forge and force rules down on their followers that they themselves will never touch nor taste punishment for breaking. They create covenants of cowardice and cunning, meant more to rule rubes and ravenous religious rats, all devouring the message as they listen to their protector's pipe play a tune. A song of sin and simple-minded stupidity that numbs and turns them to nothing but a herd of pissing donkeys to be prodded and poked in a direction of their herd master's choosing.

Those rules—covenants of kings—are etched in the blood of those sent to die for their making, impaling themselves on words of wisdom and wonder from beings that carry not compassion nor crowing cock for those who would be ruled.

Of all this I told you I would relay only the simple truth. For I had yet in my life then, nor have I ever since, been nailed to a cross nor burned alive for telling my story. And yet . . . there *are* those who have been. So when I relate this next part, you can rest assured that it's nothing . . . save my great God's honest truth.

Lilith. . . My mind couldn't wrap itself completely around the evil of it. "Eve" stood a few feet beneath a hovering and self-satisfied, bright Life. And the arena was once again packed with my Great Mother's minions. Maybe they had never left? I'd never know.

But looking at them all. . . Dictators in the eternities of the Garden would only dream of rivaling her success at packing a stadium with as many blind bats to follow them into darkness.

The plan for my existence was clear: I was damned to be a continuous spectacle for her feathered fans' amazement as well as their whipped-to-frenzy anger. But the most damning thing of all was that Adam stood resurrected next to Eve, just as zombified and seemingly oblivious to his own incineration just hours before.

Two Golden Guardians, Life's pit vipers of poison and pain, came down into the dungeons and ripped Eve and me from our individual cells. They dragged us to the arena where the Man-monkey, Adam, and my great God waited. The grandstands were filled with Life's adoring fans.

I steeled myself for what would come. I was actually a bit excited to get a chance to "couple" with my beautiful God one last time. I truly believed that to show off her own power, she'd have to attempt to kill me herself. And when she did, I'd wrap my fists around her throat such that no more lies would ever escape her miserable mouth again.

Black oil on fire could not describe the inferno that raged just beneath my breast. My hearts burned for revenge. Redress for my birth into a life as lost as it was. Retribution for being violated by my own God's lascivious lust. Retaliation for the rough and raping treatment of the waif that was now Eve. And recompense for a fallen God, Eden, who clearly to me now had harbored only hope and happiness for her Garden, despite her lack of will to fight her own creation's temptation.

Life's fanfare was her own light, and she shined it as brightly as she could until the entire stadium gasped and recoiled. Searing heat burst the stadium to spectacle. I leaned into the burning discomfort of the radiating bright on my skin. Fire, it seemed, had become my ferocious friend. For it didn't burn me as it once had, and my skin turned back white from its slowly braising cooked-red color.

Life neither paid attention nor noticed this. She was more concerned with the huge rock tablets that two of her newest sex slave serpents held up for her to read. "As the great Garden of Life has narrowly escaped falling into ruin," she raised her voice to booming and blasting all throughout the stadium, "and as precious daughter and mother and any sons or daughters they might have bore are no *more!* And as certain as the Garden lies barren and teetering on the brink of being bastardized by your own *brethren!*"

The roar shot up through the grandstands even as the tidal wave of testaments against me swelled and crest at their peak. It was of little matter to me, as any dousing damnation she sought to pour over me I could match with the hatred of my fire.

Life continued even as the clamor in the grandstands barely died down. "*I*," she shouted over the stirring screeches and they stopped, "your Great God Mother, *Life*, have decreed that there shall be covenants to protect all the gardens to come. Secure them from the rape and ruin with which they have begun."

And a cheering—the likes of clamor which I've only seen since at injuring jousts and gutting gladiator festivals of sword and shield, set upon brother to draw precious blood for the sport of those who would never feel the sting of steel—shot sound up through the grand-stands and bounced back off the huge domed roof.

Life motioned to one of her closest Golden Guardians, and stone tablets were brought by two others and placed in front of him so that he might read them. My eyes widened but a little. She would not even deliver her own lies, preferring to let the bile fall from the lips of her. . . Who this one was, I didn't know. I knew it was not Norl. Norl was in the black with my lost Lilith's soul.

Yet any great spectacle, run by self-aggrandizing sinners would have to begin with introductions. Gods loved to hear the names of their sons and daughters spoken in front of their followers.

"Michael?" Life said his name as she had said mine not six days earlier. And as she was my witness, I would not allow the sun to set on the seventh. "Michael," she said again, "the commander of your Lord's army of angels in Heaven, will stand for you in this great time of conflict, my children. And he'll read contract and covenant for the

Garden, its inhabitants and every angel in the Heavens."

Michael, for his part in it, was content to smile and nod his head at Life. Something I was content to do, not 6 days before.

Life looked down beside her at him and smiled back. I knew the expression, and imagined that Michael's snakes had taken the place of mine, buried in the womb of his Great Mother, attempting to subvert my own seed. "Michael," she said yet again as if she just wanted me to hear it spew from her lips, "let laws fall from lips, and have us be done with this day of damnation."

"Michael" wasted little time. A chopped-hard block of wood he looked to be, with dark scalp and blue eyes to rival my own. A more seriously faced or sinuously muscled angel I've only seen in my meanest eternity since. Yet as replacement for fair Steg? I thought not. "The serpent, Steg," he shouted at the tablets, "for having offended the Lord your God who brought you out of the darkness—out of the house of the black bondage. . . It is hereby decreed that none shall have any other gods before Life."

That first commandment? Knowing what I do now, that was what they were. Yet the first one hardly needed to be written down, for I don't believe there was a wing in the grandstands who didn't fear its detachment were that rule to be broken. I certainly had not.

And yet Michael would accuse otherwise. "And for having worshipped false idols of the sun and sand and sky and stars," he said, "for having carved an image in his own mind—the likeness of fire, bowing down to serve it. . . As your God is a jealous god, she shall visit this iniquity upon you to every generation of the Garden that follows, but Life shall show mercy and shine her bright kindness on those who would worship only her. All shall keep these commandments that I read to you today!"

So, the second commandment would be a truth that I thought Life incapable of telling. *Jealousy*. . . Even through the erupting crowd, I smiled at the irony of it. Jealousy was a treat saved for gods to gobble and the common geese to be gutted for merely harboring it in their hearts.

In all honesty, when I heard the third commandment, I had no recollection of my offense of it. I'd only. . . The truth? I *had* spoken it. "For taking the name of the Lord, Eden, your once God, in vain, your Lord, Life, will not hold Steg guiltless—nor any who takes *God's* name in vain from this day forward!"

The next rule, I planned to break in its entirety as soon as this "Michael" was finished with his master's miserable list. "Six days of any week you shall labor and do all your work, but the seventh day is the Sabbath of the great Lord, Life. For remember that you were a slave in the land of blackness, and the Lord your God brought you out from there by mighty hand and outstretched arm; therefore the Lord your God commands you to keep the seventh day as Sabbath."

And since that very day, I've watched deity after demagogue, dictator after destructor, decree days of non-work and worship to mark the magnitude of their own oppression. Powerful presidents and pompous piss-ant prime ministers and heads of "Panamanian" purgatories, set aside "free" days by the tens of hundreds for their minions to recover from the misery those very leaders inflict.

I shook my head. My own misery at having to listen to that brainwashed buffoon's bile as it bastardized both brethren and my own bosom, began to rival the lament over the loss of my Lilith. I looked up at Eve. She was oblivious to me. She smiled and gazed uninterrupted at Michael, listening to his speech.

"Honor your Great Mother," he continued, "as the Lord your God has commanded you, that your days may be long, and your life may be well in the land which Life is giving you."

You owe me your life, I thought to myself. That was her message, *and fear greatly, for on any given Sunday, I may decide to collect the debt for it.* It was unbelievable to me that intelligent beings would swallow putrid piss from a sewer as Michael's words spewed stench on that day.

The crowd rustled as well. I wondered if Michael could sense it, because he looked hesitantly back at Life, herself content to stare into me with her downturned grin of self-satisfied sin. When she finally felt Michael's gaze, she motioned with her hand for him to continue.

I remained silent, my rage and fire slowly growing to a bursting flame. One that I would soon unleash on this *Michael. Minion moron*, I thought.

His gums could barely keep up with the gobbling guts of the grandstands, sucking down sewage as he spoke. "For having committed all of these crimes against his brethren," Michael said, glancing at me only slightly before returning to reading, "The angel, Steg, nor any angel, Man, monkey or beast, shall not murder, shall not commit adultery, shall not steal, shall not bear false witness against their neighbor. . ."

The noise in the crowd pitched higher and the screeching turned to screaming and the flapping of wings. I'm sure a few of them, drunk on the sight and sounds of it, fell feathers-first from their perches as I've seen countless insidious idiots do on my God Life's precious Sundays.

Michael stopped spouting commandments, long enough to let any who *had* fallen, pick themselves back to their perches. By my count, he was not finished, as this list of ten—a coven of witch words . . . were missing one witch. The most wicked witch of them all.

Michael shouted above him, "And you shall not desire your neighbor's house, nor his field, nor his male servant, nor his female servant, nor ox or donkey, or *anything* that is your neighbor's."

He paused merely for effect I am certain, because the only thing of my "neighbor's" in the Garden I was guilty of coveting, stood right next to Adam, safely removed of Woman's will with which to resist him.

The tenth commandment cut into my breast and ripped out both of my hearts for all the eternities to come. For my part in it, I was as saddened and sorrowful as any angel who had participated, but I would no longer have use for my hearts after losing Lilith.

Michael faced me. He spoke from memory, as he never looked at the stone tablets his golden brethren held while he finished doing his master's bidding. "Steg," he said, "hereafter you shall be known as the father of The Fallen from your great God, Life's Heaven. And for the crime and *punishment* of coveting your neighbor's *wife* . . . you shall hereby be *stoned* . . . until you are *dead!*"

— XX —

THE FIRST STONE streaked out of the grandstands like a comet, and when it impacted the side of my face, stars shot through my eyes as if I had been blinded by Life's light. I stumbled and almost fell.

When I looked up, I was already losing some vision. Then a rock hit my mouth and several of my front teeth broke and the chips burst from my mouth. I turned to face the side of the stadium where those first two stones came from—I would not go down as a lamb! I roared at them even as rocks struck my chest and arms and knees, and I fell.

Jagged diamonds and rubies on the floor of the arena cut into my flesh, and blood flowed out onto the once shining and shimmering gemstones. I forced myself to stagger back up.

The shouting and screaming grew muffled and my vision obscured along with it, and I reached a hand towards the one my hearts were telling me was Lilith. The fire that burned over them knew she was lost to Eve. Another rock struck me in the hand and broke my finger and then my eye and I felt and heard it "pop," and pain shot into my cheek and I grabbed at my face. My hand was met with the exploded oozing remnants of a sunk-in and cracked open eye and socket. I roared above my head even as rocks rained down ruin and wrath upon every inch of my naked flesh.

And elbow and hip and back all broke beneath the increasing hail of stones. They impacted and cracked into my earthly flesh, far worse than Adam's fists had beaten me. It felt almost as heinous as the hurt in my hearts.

Midway into the rain of rocks, I fell to my knees and could not rage my way back standing. I felt a huge crack as a rock blasted the base of my back and ruptured the lowest disk in my spine. Then everything below my waist, including my long-since-ceased hissing snakes, went limp. I slumped to the side, done . . . but far from dead.

Ravens in the grandstands raged and rocks flew and some of them hit me, but many of them didn't. I slumped on my side, watching the ones that missed, thinking, *You have missed me, you miserable moronic flying monkey.*

I coughed a laugh out and spit blood, and it covered a rock that *hadn't* missed its mark. The rock now lie covered in the truth of my rage-red blood, its results spat and spilled over it.

After a time that seemed longer than my short life in the Garden, I grew numb and could no longer hear words nor whacking rock. It seemed as if the sound of rain droplets of stone was to be the last thing I would ever hear . . . before one final star exploded into my face, and my short time in that world . . . faded me back to the black.

Time ceases in the black, as the sands of it swirl like a desert storm, criss-crossing back and forth on top of itself until you are unaware which eternity is which.

I saw Lilith again, yet we were not in her Mother's great Garden. Thankfully, she was not Eve either. But the cruelty of it had not left, as she neither knew nor remembered anything from the time we spent as confidant and coveter together in the Garden.

And I am sad to say that I wish I had not seen her, for eons later— an eternity times at least five—I did see her again. Yet this time only as angry allies in purpose and plot, and not the pleasure I so desired at one time.

There were flashes of things in the Garden past and then miserable Man-monkeys that bred and bred and birthed more until I could barely keep pace. And I had become responsible for the souls of so many of the very beings I loathed. So I stoked fire into the burning flames of their misery for the sins that their forefather and my Great Mother had wrought upon me. I brought anger and affliction on them as I had felt at the hands of their gods.

I would never again have mercy or feel empathy, or compassion for pain suffered. For all those things first required my hearts to harbor even the slightest bit of love. And the last ounces of pity left in me. . . The last breath of love I had left was stoned until I was cold dead, broken beneath a sea of miniature boulders, avalanched upon it from my own brethren.

The Arena of Reckoning was the headstone for any love left in my hearts, and I didn't know it yet, but I was destined to be buried deep beneath it . . . in a fiery grave of hatred and heat.

The first sensation I had after the black . . . was warmth. And that warmth turned to heat and then to a burning greater than Life's brightness.

As I stood up, my ears burned too. Screaming and screeching, and gasping and clucking and cawing built to a flaming hot panic of pee-pissing angels in the grandstands of the arena. They all screamed, shocked and shivering and shitting themselves that I was not dead. I smiled as I stood to my full height. I had become much taller than I had been. I looked up to find Life.

Not having noticed me back on my feet, she was still smiling at her Michael. They paused as they both realized that the gasping was not, and could not be, directed toward them. They nervously glanced through the grandstands even as I stretched my shoulders into my new body.

I looked at Lilith-turned-Eve next to them, and the Man-monkey resurrected as Adam, beside all three of them. There was nothing in my hearts. I was a blank slate of a new Purgatory yet to be filled with wailing souls. Caught between a Heaven I now could not stand and a Hell I would yet create.

Even as my glorious tail returned, growing out from the base of my back, I spoke through the pain at the rebirth of it, "Hear me, my brethren," my voice boomed as both the lion and the liar I was forced to become. I spoke slowly so all of them could feel the heat of my rage build and burn at their feathers. "I will ascend from the death which you have all sent me to . . . back up here to the pit of vipers you call *Heaven!*"

And my newly gilded God's replacement, shouted over at me, "You are blasphemous in your judgment, Steg," Michael said, "to presume you may return from your death. The Lord rebuke you, serpent!"

Life fluttered in front of him, more curious than afraid of what I was saying. I don't think she fully grasped or understood the magnitude of what my returning from certain death meant. Her big black eyes widened slightly—surprise more than concern crept across her face. She motioned her hand in front of Michael and he tilted his head down at her. Then she fluttered closer.

I raised my long arm at her and pointed my finger. As I did, I noticed that I had become more crimson creature than pale white-skinned snake. And my talon slowly pushed itself all the way out. I had little control over it. "For your great God," I spoke harshly even as my face contorted at speaking her name, "Life has defiled all of you in her deceptions! She has slain monkey and mother and daughter alike, and now she will have *my* judgment and face demon as he builds new Hell to house her children!"

She flew closer. Her bright light grew brighter and the grandstands squawked at it, but I didn't shy away. I welcomed the heat of Life as a warm fire to blanket my cold hearts.

The pain struck me before I realized what caused it. I fell to my knees and growled and roared out. Then my once lost and forgotten wings ripped through the flesh along the sides of my spine, and mangled meat and bloody chunks fell from my back.

A few of the more weak-willed of her followers scrambled from their perches and flew toward the roof of the arena. I watched them hover just beneath it as if they were pet pigeons waiting for their "god" to open the latch to their cage.

Life raised up her hand and several of their brothers took flight toward them. When they reached the panicked deserters, talons and teeth grasped and gnashed at them, and then flew them back into the grandstands, dragging them by their wings. There would be no escape for anyone. No one would ever leave a dictator's gathering until they were dismissed.

I let Life know what her precious new rule in the eternities to come would look and feel like. Because if I was certain of anything, she could claw and kill me a million times and I would come back for more.

I turned my back to her and faced the opposite side of the grandstands. Then I stretched my dripping red wings out wide, and I flapped up into the middle of the arena. I hovered as I spoke. "Above the stars of this God I will set my own throne," I said. "I will sit on every mountain of misery in the far reaches of the Garden; I will ascend above the heights of the sin-covered clouds of your God's lies; I will make myself most high above her treachery and taint. And I will not bow to benevolent bitch"—I turned toward her. She hovered up slowly. I looked down past her at Michael on the floor of the arena, and I pointed—"nor blaspheming bastard, spewing her vile bile of lies!"

She was letting me dig my own grave with her followers, but I cared not. They could bury me wherever they wanted—I would resurrect to shine the wicked evil truth back at them—a raging red mirror of hatred for all to see and feel her deceit.

I knew she would annihilate me at the end of it—she would have no choice. Yet I knew what she might only sense, it would make no difference. My death and damnation would only serve to place fear in the hearts of her followers. And I would use that fear to urinate on their disbelief until it festered to infected flesh and bone.

I little time left to tease and taunt her to follow me . . . before she would have to break her own precious "Sabbath day" commandment, proving herself hypocrite . . . if only for my own self-satisfaction.

"Now is the judgment of this world," I spoke loudly, but ceased shouting, for we were almost to the place I wanted Life—barely able to contain her own boiling fury. "And *now* . . . the true ruler of this world will be cast out by your all-powerful Mother. She shall abort her firstborn child before your very eyes."

I knew I would not be the last baby that Life would murder. For by the time the eternities ended, she would most likely kill thousands, millions to satisfy her lust for lies instead of liberty. I waited for the scalpel of her lightning to cut me from the womb of her wasting world . . . one final time. I almost smiled as I gave her one final push. "And for her sin of sedition against her own sister," I said, "I shall spike her first child's hands and feet to a post, and he shall die festering next to filthy thieves and beggars."

I was blustering at the time—taunting her to attack me—but knowing what I do now. . . Well, I shall leave that for the final testament of my fallen faithful friends to relate.

I fluttered down past her and landed on the floor of the arena, resisting all temptation to rip her lying lungs out so she might not speak more untruths. She'd set the rules for the game and I would follow them to the ends of the eternities if need be, but she would not beat me with my own tail again.

Life fluttered and followed me back down. I could feel her, smiling behind me. There was little time left. I could see that Adam and Eve had not departed, and if the black had let me go at the time I had thought. . . If the pair of them didn't leave soon they would risk having to complete their "work" on my Great Mother's bloody Sabbath Sunday. Then where would her covenants be?

"How you shall fall from heaven," Life finally shouted, "oh Day Star, my Son of the Morning! How you are cut down to the ground as Satan. You who would seek to lie your own brothers low! I shall form a great pit beneath us and we shall bury you in a sea of fire beside an endless lake of flames and fury, so you might feel the burning truth of your own treachery!"

Then the roof of the arena made a great grinding metal against metal noise as it slowly rotated open. And I saw a single golden angel float down from the Heaven above it. He held in his hand a great iron key on a great chain. And then ten Golden Guardians seized me as a slayer might seize a dragon.

I offered no resistance, only giving back a mischievous smile as protest for their harsh handling of my now flickering and flaming wings. My fire burned into them and I could smell the sweetness of their burned feathers.

Once they had me, Life delivered her sentence. "Sinful serpent, Steg, who is now devil as Satan," she said, "I bind you for all the eternities—a thousand if need be. We in the name of truth, throw you into the pit as a viper with your lies. And I shall shut and seal it over you, so that you might not deceive the angels in Heaven nor Man in the Garden any longer this—" And then I think she figured it out, because even the monkey minions in the grandstands had sensed that the clock had clicked over to the seventh day.

And there was nothing she could do to stop it. Leaving me living among her minions for a full day more would risk one of them doubting or discovering the truth that she needed to bury with me.

Even as the angel carrying the key hefted it high above his head for all in the arena to see, Life's face grew cold and blank. She was powerless to stop him from using the key's weight to enslave me.

When the cheering died down, the angel pushed the key—he had some difficulty doing it—down into the floor at the center of the arena. Then he used the entirety of his body to wrestle and wrench that great key, twisting it to the right until the entire hall could not mistake the loud clanking and banging of metal dungeon doors unlocking.

The angel raced backward, not even pausing to remove the key. And flames shot into the center of the arena, fifty feet at least into the air. And the heat as the floor opened up was like a blast from a hot furnace as fire and fury escaped.

"Great Satan," Life shouted at me, "this shall be your punishment for sins committed in hatred." She was in the throes of the crowd now —to stop it would be folly.

She knew, as I do now, that even as she broke her own commandment, there was no authority that would dare bring her to trial or judgment for it. As I've told you, such is the privilege of being a god.

"You shall suffer ten billion deaths as a dark angel," she screeched at me. "For even as you were once of the light of Life, so now shall none know you lived. Of this I promise you." I wondered if she even realized the lie as she told it.

And though I offered no resistance, the ten angels holding my limbs and tail lifted me and carried me to the edge of the opening pit of flame and fire.

They inched as close as they dared, lest their own bodies and beaks burn and their blood boil along with me. And they threw me at the ground toward the flaming entrance to the pit below, but I didn't roll into it. Instead, I stood up to more gasps from the grandstands.

The fear of my benevolent brothers was misplaced, as I would only offer the sting of insult as my final goodbye. A last salute to a Great Mother who was anything but. I got what I came for—Life and I knew the truth of it. She was a hypocritical hound of a Hell she believed she condemned only me to live. Yet she would share that dungeon of damnation with me soon enough.

"Great Life," I shouted back at her, "my birth Mother in Heaven. Your loins shall forever swelter in sorrow at the loss of the company of my snakes. And in your suffering you'll most surely send insult and injury toward me as hate. Yet as I am your most beautiful angel—your first child of lust and love—you shall never be able to forget me.

"No other name shall pass your lips at the throes of his thrusts. So sweet and sinful my name shall be to your ears, yet it will only exist in the past of your mind." And I looked up at the grandstands and let them all feel what true freedom looked like.

For what is freedom, but the courage to look in the face of lies and deceit and death and spit the truth back into its mouth? "Ten thousand names of your replacements shall whisper in your ears, and a million rough and raw hands shall claw at your hips . . . but you shall never know another sound sweeter, nor a touch more tender than that of *Lucifer* . . . your true Son of the Morning!"

And before she could respond or I could drink in her understanding that I was telling the truth, the Mother that had birthed me into her twisted and treacherous nightmare of living, watched me pitch myself into the fiery flames and disappear over the edge into the depths of the pit, effectively aborting myself from my Great Mother, Life.

That is my story. Not testament, but tale of how I reclaimed my own whip from the monster who took it. Not what you may have expected, I am certain, given the infectious disease that those who would seek to edify and educate you afflict you with each day. Lies you have no doubt been fed your entire life.

What misery it must be to walk as a Man-monkey, shitting and pissing your way through your existence without clue or concern to the truth of the lies that surround you. I am still amazed by your immunity to it. If truth were a vile viper's venom, upon striking you, its fangs would crack and break upon the steel rod of your misguided belief . . . as mine have *so* many times.

Alas, thankfully, I have patience . . . and all the time in the eternities to teach you. For now, you should take time to study testaments of those who have actually seen the truth first hand, for one day—and this is truly the only way anyone will believe me—you shall most surely feel Life's wrath for yourself.

— XXI —

Life put the ruby red apple to her lips and smelled deeply. Then she opened her jaws, wider than Michael was comfortable seeing, and ate the entirety of the fruit in one bone crushing crunch. The slightest ounce of nectar slipped its way free of the corner of her mouth and trickled down her chin. She quickly wiped it with the tip of her longest finger and offered it to Michael.

The archangel Michael, strong and powerful as he was, had seen and meted out punishment for tasting of the poison apples of the Garden. And he wanted no part in the misery and destruction that they had wrought on the archangel, Steg.

Seeking to delay finding out for himself, he hesitated with a question, "You had precious poison of fruit from. . .? It has been within your grasp this entire week?"

Life smiled at him. She would drink in *his* poison soon enough. "Simple"—she licked her lips, finishing off any other droplet that might have escaped her jaws—"and *sinfully* delicious, Michael, no mere fruit can pump and press poison into a Man-monkey's heart. Such vile venom must be boiled and brewed and burned into his soul. With the ferocity of his own guilt over sin he must be poisoned." She chuckled at her own words.

Michael moved his head back away from her finger.

"Regret and loss and misery," Life continued, "are its cauldron, and Man's mind alone is the wooden ladle with which it is stirred to an infectious ink. Left to himself—absent guilt and shame—my beautiful Man would simply . . . blissfully exist in his glorious Garden, spewing his own excrement over its entirety."

Michael's face scrunched ever so slightly, though from Life's words or the fear of the single drop of nectar on her finger, only he knew.

Life kept her finger in front of his face, challenging him to escape it. "And *that*, dear Michael, would provide neither torment nor joy of observing it. The only product of Man would be precious piss and pomposity—an absolute mess in my Garden . . . for no apparent Protector's purpose or pause at enjoyment."

Delay was all Michael had. He'd seen enough of the results of defiance for one lazy Sunday. "They . . . seem to be making a disaster of it despite—"

"Ahh," said Life, "and that is why I've created *you* fairer than Lucifer, Michael. Shall we retire to pass the eternities witnessing that destruction from your God's . . . *throne* then?" She turned, yet her finger didn't move from in front of Michael's face. "No?" she asked in front of her. "Very well." And she whipped her finger to her own lips and sucked it clean of any hint that the apple's juice had ever thought to escape her. Whether it was poison or plump treat, only she and her fallen angel would ever know.

Life turned brighter in anticipation, and she fluttered her wings. She floated up the steps to her newly conquered chambers, as effortlessly as she had manipulated her latest fallen angel to win them for her.

Michael followed, only flaps behind her. His God's bidding invitation was neither question nor request.

Life mused to herself, smiling in front of her as Michael followed behind. *Fair Lucifer*, she thought, *you would have bitten favored finger from hand . . . had I offered it so. I shall miss that of you.*

It was the last truth she would tell herself of the sin and treachery in Eden's Garden. . . The truth of Steg, and the knowledge that sooner or later . . . sin touches every god.

END OF PROLOGUE

Congratulations! You just finished *STEG*, the prologue novella to Steve Windsor's *THE FALLEN* series.

Turn the page to find out how you can get the first novel in the series, *JUMP*. >>>>>

JUMP

THE FALLEN: TESTAMENT 1

STEVE WINDSOR

Take a front-row seat in a lively afterlife!

Relax and enter an exquisitely created universe you'll thank your own God you're not a part of. But you can't help but want to get to know those who are.

Most of us have been taught a version of the war between Heaven and Hell. In *JUMP: The Fallen - Testament 1*, Steve Windsor offers up a decidedly dystopian look at a version of that ultimate showdown you'd never enter voluntarily, and does so in beautifully drawn, fleshed-out prose that escorts you there, plops you down in a front-row seat in the "Arena of Reckoning," and makes you want to stay for the finish. As a spectator, of course.

This superbly-written first entry in *The Fallen* series begins in a Seattle you'll recognize even if you've never been there: cool, cloudy, overcast, rainy - and dark. Keep your eyes on that last one, because you're going to see a lot of it. You don't stay in Seattle. You travel far beyond into an infinity you first wish you didn't have to, but soon come to know you're meant to, until you desperately want to. Windsor's writing is so intense, so achingly, mind-blowingly real that you'll have to remind yourself this is a book. And you're not going to want to put it down for a second until the finish.

And thank God - or the Devil, or whoever's running things in this eternity, that this is just book one. So sprout your wings and save your seat; the ride's just beginning.

Jake Blake lives in a world the likes of which your great-great grandkids—if the population projection Windsor gives pans out—may face if the author's social, political and economic dystopia has even a tad of a chance of forming for real. A "citizen" and former agent of a government that makes "1984" look like a spring festival, Jake finds himself on the receiving end of this world's obsession with catching those who've hidden guns. Private firearms are forbidden. Period. Not just forbidden but undeniably, undoubtedly, decisively, distinctly, clearly, positively forbidden. And after initially playing the role of enforcer, Jake isn't having it anymore.

The reader is taken for a wild ride—or fall, as Windsor would have it—from Seattle high-rises to an afterlife where showdowns between good and evil are presented as not just war but the ultimate showmanship. Individual judgments take place in an arena with spectators. The Gods are expected to put on a good show and Windsor makes sure they do so.

Windsor's characterization is nothing less than brilliant. Jake can be called your hero but he's really your anti-hero. You end up rooting for him in spite of yourself. You realize early on that earthly life has become a world where Uncle Sam has metamorphosed into Uncle Satan, where the "Protection" squad consists of "the State's personal pit bulls of justice," where the rights of citizens were allowed to dissipate a long time ago, and where Jake's emotions are merely "a hop, skip and a jump to pissed off." Compared with most of his descriptions, that's gentle. He's not a happy camper, and regardless of where on a moral compass you put him, you wouldn't be either.

It doesn't take long for Jake, and the story, to sprout wings in a lively afterlife that perches the reader in a secure spot even while falling. You get a uniquely idiosyncratic version of the all-powerful "Life"—God, Supreme Being, whatever you want to call this ultimate entity, and also of the Devil or "Dal," the "Dark Angel of Light." And you get it with language that stays with you. Jake's priceless exchange with a momentarily forgetful Dal leaves you howling for more: "Leave it to me to arrive in Hell on the day the Devil gets Alzheimer's."

Much of what the millions of angel-spectators in the Arena of Reckoning witness is the "eternal" bickering between these two rulers of Heaven and Hell. Enjoy that worldly exchange while the story of the supremely skeptical Jake, who calls Dal "a conspiracy ranter after my own heart," and his family takes center stage. And again, notwithstanding his glaring cynicism and constant colorful cussing—or perhaps because of it—you find yourself rooting for this anti-hero and his far-more-moral wife and daughter for, let us say, a favored place in perpetuity.

Finally given a bit of power, Jake's gutting for revenge. Everyone who hurt him and his family has it coming. You root for him a tad less here, but you quickly pick it up again. Throughout the story you find yourself caring for this immensely flawed character whose four-letter words add a tangy flavor to the hills and halls of eternity. Not because what he does is good, but because Windsor has made him and those around him eminently ... human. For the reader, the challenge in *JUMP* is not what Jake has to contend with, but putting the effing book down to get to sleep at night.

Ana - (Amazon Review)

GET BOOK 1

THE FALLEN series begins in *JUMP : Testament 1*.
Get your copy of *JUMP* before anyone else.

vixenink.com/jump-fallen/

THE FALLEN Series of Religious Thrillers:
JUMP, FURY, FAITH, HOLE, DOGG, BURN, LIVED, LIFE, RAIN, SALVATION

Oh, and one more thing >>>

I smile and remember my Great Mother's reaction when she birthed me from the black.

Not what you expected, I'd wager. Then again, what did you think I would look like? Be thankful you can't see my hands. Claws tend to scare even the stoutest of you. But truth is like that—hard to reconcile what you've been taught with what . . . *is*. No matter—there is a method to all madness.

The Lake of Fire. . . I stare at the burning flames and smile, thinking of the anguish and misery I will use to bring them all to it. Any Man-monkey I can get my claws into will learn the error of their own beliefs. The task will be . . . difficult.

However, I have nothing but everlasting life—as you well know by now—and the eternal knowledge that the apples of the Garden gave me.

"Lucifer. . ." I mutter to myself. I bet naming myself *that* surprised her. But I would not spend one more day in my eternal life wearing the monicker *she* gave me. *Steg*, I think, gazing across the vast ocean of black and orange flames. *Never again will I. . .* "Hello. . ." I shout it loud enough that if there were anyone here, my voice would leave no doubt that their new master had arrived.

But the lake and the deep blackness surrounding it echo back only the sound of my own voice. *That just will not do*, I think to myself. That's *her* way not mine. I prefer things a little more . . . controversial. Time to get a few souls down here in the pit with me.

Because to be sure, this is no warm and wonderful Garden of Eden with Lilith. This is the heat of fire and brimstone down here, and I've had enough of the gorgeous green envy and tyrannical treachery in Eden's Garden to last me an eternity. No, from here, things will be . . . different.

Time to procure some wailing souls to share their "thoughts" down here with me.

If you haven't guessed by now, this is an invitation. Curious? You should be. I thought you aught to at least experience both sides of the story before passing judgment, however. So now that you have, it would be most appreciated if you clicked your way over to Amazon and left a helpful review of my tale.

I smile as my true *tail* flicks the rocks behind me. *That will be an interesting . . . revelation.*

Thank you,

Lucifer, "Son" of the Morning

About Amazon Bestselling Author
Steve Windsor

Steve Windsor is the author of the *THE FALLEN* series of religious suspense thrillers. STEG, *JUMP, FURY, FAITH, HOLE, DOGG, BURN, LIVED, LIFE, RAIN*, and *SALVATION*.

He lives with his wife and two daughters in the real world . . . and many, many other cool people in the imaginary world in his mind.

Connect with the author:
EMAIL: steve@vixenink.com
FACEBOOK: vixenink.com/facebook-page

Thank you so much for reading *STEG*.

"I write fiction novels, because the truth . . . is just way too scary."
—Steve Windsor - Amazon Bestselling Author